The legend at work...

A kiss on the lips the bargain will seal, and undying love will the couple soon feel.

This can't be true, Maddy thought. She forced a nervous laugh. "You're right. It was something your grandma made up." She and Pete hadn't kissed. They had nothing to worry about.

"What is it? What does it say?" He tried to grab the paper, but she held it back and out of his reach. She tried to scoot away, but Pete lunged for her, grabbing her gently and pinning her down with his body.

Pete no longer seemed interested in the paper. His lips were just inches away from hers. His intention reflected clearly in his eyes, and Maddy panicked. "Pete, wait! Don't do it! You don't under—"

"Sorry, Maddy, but I've got to." He covered her mouth with his own.

Dear Reader,

It's February—the month of love. And what better way to celebrate Valentine's Day than with a Harlequin American Romance novel.

This month's selection begins with the latest installment in the RETURN TO TYLER series. *Prescription for Seduction* is what Darlene Scalera offers when sparks fly between a lovely virgin and a steadfast bachelor doctor. *The Bride Said, "Surprise!"* is another of Cathy Gillen Thacker's THE LOCKHARTS OF TEXAS, and is a tender tale about a secret child who brings together two long-ago lovers. (Watch for Cathy's single title, *Texas Vows: A McCabe Family Saga*, next month from Harlequin Books.)

In Millie Criswell's charming new romance, *The Pregnant Ms. Potter* is rescued from a blizzard by a protective rancher who takes her into his home—and into his heart. And in *Longwalker's Child* by Debra Webb, a proud Native American hero is determined to claim the child he never knew existed, but first he has to turn the little girl's beautiful guardian from his sworn enemy into his loving ally.

So this February, treat yourself to all four of our wonderful Harlequin American Romance titles. And in March, look for Judy Christenberry's *Rent a Millionaire Groom*, the first book in Harlequin American Romance's new promotion, 2001 WAYS TO WED.

Wishing you happy reading,

Melissa Jeglinski
Associate Senior Editor
Harlequin American Romance

THE PREGNANT MS. POTTER

Millie Criswell

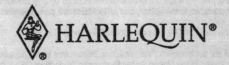

HARLEQUIN®

TORONTO • NEW YORK • LONDON
AMSTERDAM • PARIS • SYDNEY • HAMBURG
STOCKHOLM • ATHENS • TOKYO • MILAN • MADRID
PRAGUE • WARSAW • BUDAPEST • AUCKLAND

ISBN 0-373-16863-2

THE PREGNANT MS. POTTER

ABOUT THE AUTHOR

Millie Criswell didn't start out to be a writer. Her greatest aspiration in life was to tap dance with the Rockettes. However, when that failed to work out, she put pen to paper and has authored eighteen bestselling, award-winning historical, category and contemporary romances. She has won numerous awards, including the *Romantic Times* Career Achievement Award, *Reviewer's Choice* Award and the Maggie Award from Georgia Romance Writers. Millie has two grown children and resides with her husband in Virginia.

Books by Millie Criswell

HARLEQUIN AMERICAN ROMANCE
810—THE WEDDING PLANNER
863—THE PREGNANT MS. POTTER

HARLEQUIN HISTORICALS
508—THE MARRYING MAN

Don't miss any of our special offers. Write to us at the following address for information on our newest releases.

Harlequin Reader Service
U.S.: 3010 Walden Ave., P.O. Box 1325, Buffalo, NY 14269
Canadian: P.O. Box 609, Fort Erie, Ont. L2A 5X3

The Taggart
Wedding Ring Quilt Legend

Place this quilt upon your bed

and in one month you shall be wed.

But if you think you'd rather not,

Then a spinster's life shall be your lot.

A man and a woman who meet if by chance,

Will soon be doing the marital dance.

A kiss on the lips the bargain will seal,

And undying love will the couple soon feel.

—Grandma Maggie Taggart

Chapter One

Maddy Potter didn't think her life could get any worse.

Ha! What did she know? It wasn't bad enough that she was eight weeks pregnant without a husband in sight—"Stupid! Stupid! Stupid!" Now she was stranded in the middle of Nowhere, Colorado, in the clutches of a snowstorm—a whiteout, the radio had called it—and her chances of reaching her sister's house in Leadville seemed non-existent.

"Don't even think about driving in this storm, little lady," the car rental agent had told her two hours before. "Get yourself a nice warm hotel room somewhere near the airport and ride it out. It's the sensible thing to do."

"Of course, when have I ever been sensible?" Maddy asked herself. Surely not when she had allowed passion to override good judgment and had given in to David Lassiter's persistent pursuit, engaging in unprotected sex for the first time in her life. Well, not exactly unprotected. They had used a condom, but the damn thing broke right in the middle of everything. Just her luck.

Stupid wasn't really a strong enough sentiment to sum up how she felt about her behavior. Asinine was probably a better word. Or how about insane? That fit nicely, too.

Heaving a sigh, Maddy's hand moved to her belly, and she felt the tiny life growing inside her—David's child. But David Lassiter was her boss at Lassiter, Owens and Cumberland, the third largest advertising firm in New York City, not her boyfriend, and certainly not her fiancé. He'd made it clear that he wasn't looking for any entanglements, including, and most especially, a wife.

Not that she was anxious to get married, either.

She'd been doing fine on her own. Wonderful, in fact! She didn't need a man to complicate things, to view her as competition, or worse, the little woman.

But she thought it only fair that the father of her child be informed of his impending fatherhood. When she'd confided to David that she was pregnant, he hadn't wasted any time in pulling out his checkbook and offering her a substantial amount of money for an abortion.

"Unfeeling bastard!" she muttered, thinking back to the smug look on his face. If he hadn't been such a jerk, threatening her with her job and making it clear that there was no room in his life for a child, she wouldn't have run off like a frightened teenager two weeks before Christmas to seek comfort in the arms of the one person she knew she could count on: her older sister, Mary Beth.

And it sure as heck hadn't been sensible to drive through a snowstorm knowing how little experience she had operating a car in such conditions. She lived in New York City, for heaven's sake! What did she know about driving? She took taxis and the subway when she needed to get somewhere; she didn't even own a car.

"Well, Maddy, you dolt! You've really gone and done it this time." The snow was piled so thickly on the windshield that she couldn't see a foot in front of her, let alone the surrounding countryside. She knew only that she'd taken Highway 24 from the airport in Colorado Springs—Denver's Stapleton had been closed due to the storm—and an hour later had taken a wrong turn onto a secondary road, hit a patch of icy pavement and careened into a ditch when she'd foolishly applied the brakes too hard. One of the front wheels had come off and the car was listing to one side. It was not driveable and the rental people were not going to be pleased—if, in fact, she ever saw them or anyone again. At this point she had her doubts.

"Okay, God, I need a little help here. It's true, I screwed up, but now I need your help. This precious baby growing inside me shouldn't be punished for my stupidity. I admit what I did was wrong, so give me a break."

Maddy glanced down at the red leather purse on the seat next to her—a Coach bag, the symbol of her success. She remembered how happy she'd been when she had finally earned enough money to buy it.

Not that such things mattered now. Nothing mattered now except surviving.

Reaching into her purse, she extracted her cellular phone, wondering if it still worked, praying it did. If she could reach her sister, Mary Beth's husband, Lyle, could come fetch her. Lyle was smart and sensible—the salt-of-the-earth type. He'd know what to do.

Grateful the phone's battery appeared to be working, she punched in the Randolph's number and hit send. It started ringing at once, and she breathed a sigh of relief.

Her spurt of excitement was short-lived, however, for when the call was answered, it wasn't Mary Beth or Lyle, but a female operator. "I'm sorry but your call cannot be completed as dialed. Please hang up and dial again."

She did, twelve different times. And twelve different times she got the same message. Then the phone conked out completely.

Maddy wasn't the type of woman who usually gave in to tears. She was the take-charge type, always in control of a situation, and a damn good advertising executive. Of course, she'd never been stranded in the middle of a blizzard with nothing to eat—her stomach grumbled, making it abundantly clear that it wanted to be fed; a useless cell phone—she tossed the offending object into the back seat;

and a bladder that was full to bursting—she crossed her ankles and gritted her teeth.

Then she started singing at the top of her lungs. Maddy always sang when she was nervous. She began with *Silent Night,* then moved on to *Santa Claus is Coming to Town,* and ended with a screeching chorus of *O Holy Night* that would have made a dog howl had there been one in the vicinity. But the festive songs hadn't made her predicament any more bearable. If anything, they made it worse, for she realized she just might not make it until Christmas. And that made her mad.

"Okay, God, you've had your laugh. Now, how about helping me out? I said I was sorry. I admitted to being stupid. What more do you want?"

It was at that low point when she thought she would surely die of exposure—you couldn't keep your engine idling or you'd die of carbon monoxide poisoning, she knew that much—when a light suddenly flashed through her windshield.

The beam was muted because of the snow, but it appeared to be from headlights, truck headlights, if she wasn't mistaken. The roar of the diesel engine was distinctive. She knew about diesel engines because she'd once designed an ad campaign for Ford Motor Company.

"Hello!" a male voice called out, becoming clearer as her rescuer approached the vehicle. "Is anyone there?"

Heart pounding, she banged on the driver's side window. "Yes! I'm here! Please help me!" She tried to open the door, but the snow piled against it made that impossible.

He banged twice on the roof, she thought to re-assure her, for which she was grateful. "Hang on. I'm coming around the other side of the car. I'll try to get the door open. Looks like you've busted an axel." A few moments later, and not without a great deal of cursing, he pried open the door.

Maddy breathed a sigh of relief. "Thank you, God!" she mouthed, blinking back tears and scooting toward the man standing there. He was tall, blue eyed and covered with snow, and she'd never seen any-thing or anyone look so wonderful.

PETE TAGGART SHOOK HIS HEAD as he helped the woman out of her vehicle. She had on high heels—high heels, for Pete's sake!—a navy-blue suit with little gold buttons, and a raincoat that may have had a woolen liner in it, but he couldn't be certain. Based on what he'd seen so far, he doubted it.

City girl, he thought, curling his lip disdainfully.

"You'll never be able to walk in those shoes, ma'am. Put your arms around my neck, and I'll carry you to the truck."

She shook her head. "That's n-not ne-neces... cessary." The woman's teeth were chattering. "I c-can man-manage."

"Dammit! Of course, it's necessary, or I wouldn't have said so. Now quit being stubborn and do as I say, or we're both going to freeze to death."

Since the snow was nearly up to her knees, she

finally nodded and held out her arms. With ease, he lifted her, but it took a lot more concentration and muscle to maneuver his way back to the pickup. The snow had drifted several feet in some places, making the going slow and arduous.

When they finally reached the three-quarter-ton truck, he lifted her onto the front bench seat, slammed the door shut and seated himself behind the wheel. "You're lucky I came down this road this afternoon, or you'd probably have frozen to death. The road's private and doesn't get much in the way of traffic. And the way your car looks you won't be driving it for awhile."

"Th-thank you," she managed, holding her hands out to the heater vent. The hot air pricked her skin like needles as it thawed her hands. "I didn't mean to trespass. I was on my way to my sister's in Leadville, and I guess I took a wrong turn."

He whistled. "Leadville? You're hell and gone from Leadville. You're on Taggart land, ma'am. I'm Pete Taggart, owner of this cattle ranch."

The pride in his voice was unmistakable. She'd heard pride like that voiced by her own father many times before. She wasn't impressed then, and she wasn't now. "I don't really know how I ended up here."

"It's easy to lose your bearings during a whiteout. I'm just glad I was checking on my ornery bull, Henry, and had reason to come this far from the house."

She found it endearing that he named his animals.

Maybe he wasn't such a hard-ass after all. Maddy forced a smile, though her frozen face felt as if it would crack from the effort. "I'm Madeline Potter, but most people call me Maddy."

He kept his eyes riveted on the road in front of him as he talked. "Whatever possessed you to drive in weather like this? A person should have more sense than that. Of course, women don't."

Maddy stiffened, unable to believe what she was hearing. "I beg your pardon?"

"You heard me right. Most women don't have a lick of sense when it comes to practical things, like the elements. Like wearing proper clothing and shoes." He gazed at her high heels once again and shook his head, not bothering to hide his disdain. "Looks like you're one of *those* women."

The heat flaming her cheeks and body had Maddy thawing out quickly. "I'm an advertising executive from New York City, I'll have you know. And I'm extremely intelligent. I graduated with honors from Vassar." She wouldn't waste her breath telling him about having to work three jobs simultaneously on top of the heavy class load she carried, or the numerous loans she'd taken out to achieve her goal. She doubted Cowboy Pete would give a hoot or a holler.

"Is that so? And did they teach you at Vassar to drive through blizzards and risk your fool neck?" Pete knew he was being unreasonably hard—he didn't know the woman, after all—but he had good reasons. The best of reasons.

"What they taught me was to be independent, which I am. And to compete in a man's world, which I've done, quite successfully, thank you very much. They also taught me about male chauvinists who don't like women. Men such as yourself, Mr. Taggart."

"Oh, I like women just fine, Miz Potter, ma'am," he replied, exaggerating the feminist moniker. "I like 'em hot, naked and under me."

Maddy swallowed her gasp, her lips thinning. "You, Mr. Taggart, are…are…never mind. You just are." She didn't want to anger the Neanderthal and find herself dumped back out in the snow, so she kept her unflattering opinion to herself. She doubted a man with a head as thick as a tree trunk would listen anyway.

Pete grinned, noting the heightened color to her cheeks. "I suspect so, ma'am. But I know when to come out of the rain, or, in this case, snow."

"I admit it was foolish of me to attempt driving to Mary Beth's house during the storm, but I was anxious to see my sister. And I wasn't planning on getting lost or having my car skid off the road."

"Hit the brakes, did you? Didn't your daddy ever teach you never to hit the brakes during a skid?"

Maddy counted silently to ten, unclenched her teeth and said, "My *daddy,* as you refer to my father, Mr. Taggart, was more enamored with raising his prized Duroc pigs than with raising me or my sister, or teaching us how to drive. That task fell to my mother."

Most things having to do with Maddy or Mary Beth had fallen to their mother, and it had come as no surprise when Sarah Potter's heart had finally given out, from a defective valve, the doctors had said. But Maddy felt her mother's death had really been caused by Andrew Potter's indifference and self-absorption, his total lack of awareness where others were concerned. Another grievance in a long list of grievances to heap upon her father's head.

The hurt in Maddy Potter's voice was unmistakable, so Pete backed off. The woman obviously had some unresolved issues with her old man, and he wasn't interested in hearing them.

"It's not much farther to the house. Once you've had a hot bath and hearty meal, you're going to feel a whole lot better."

A hot bath! Was the man insane? She had no intention of taking off her clothes in a stranger's house. Not that she could, even if she wanted to. Her suitcase was still in the trunk of the rental car—something she neglected to mention. "I appreciate the offer, Mr. Taggart, but I'll just use your phone, if that's all right, and be on my way. I wouldn't want to cause you any more trouble."

"Afraid that's not going to be possible, ma'am," he said, and Maddy knew a moment of fear. After all, she didn't know this man from Adam. He could be a rapist or sadistic killer, although, he certainly didn't seem to be. What he seemed to be was rude, arrogant, the Marlboro man come to life.

Nervous, she started humming *Jingle Bells,* and he

looked at her strangely. "Phone lines are down and the electricity's out. I suspect we won't have phone service again for weeks. Fir and pine trees have been snapping like twigs all morning and afternoon. And the forecast is for at least six to eight more inches of snow before morning. I don't think you'll be going anywhere for a while."

The dismay she felt reflected in her voice. "But— but my clothes are back in the car. And my sister is expecting me." That wasn't quite the truth. She'd never gotten around to calling Mary Beth. She didn't want to get into any explanations about why she was coming until she could speak to her sister in person.

It was a conversation she dreaded having. Mary Beth had always been so proud of Maddy's accomplishments, of her working her way through college and making something of herself in the business world. And Mary Beth, who desperately wanted a child, couldn't conceive one, while Maddy had had no such problem. The conversation wouldn't be easy on several levels.

"It would have been helpful, ma'am, if you'd mentioned about the clothes while we were back at the car." He didn't bother to hide his exasperation. "It's going to be a while before we can get her towed." Perhaps weeks, Pete thought. Willis Helmsley's tow truck was about as reliable as Willis, who wasn't very.

She turned her attention back to him. "I wasn't thinking beyond surviving, Mr. Taggart. I'm sorry if I've inconvenienced you."

"I'm not the one without any clothes, Miz Potter. But I'm sure we can find something for you to wear." He still had all of Bethany's clothing stored up in the attic, but he wouldn't offer her any of those garments.

Even after four years, memories of Bethany were painful. And the anger still festered like an open wound that would never heal. Pete wasn't sure he wanted it to. The anger at least made him feel alive. And it served as a constant reminder of how stubborn, self-centered and foolish women could be.

THE MULTICOLORED, four-story Victorian house stood out amidst the pristine white snow. It had been painted a buttery yellow with dark green shutters, its gingerbread trim accented in a deep cinnamon color. And it was hardly the house Maddy expected rugged rancher Pete Taggart to own. A log cabin would have suited the man much better. Or better yet—a cave!

"It looks like something out of a fairy tale," she remarked, instantly enamored of the wide wraparound front porch, which probably sported a swing in the warmer months. She secretly dreamed of owning such a house but knew her modern, efficient cubicle of a Manhattan apartment would have to do.

"Thanks. It's been in the family for generations. My great-grandmother Maggie Taggart had it built with the intention that a Taggart would always live in it."

"Then she was lucky her offspring produced males."

Pete laughed, and his face took on an entirely different appearance. With his dark hair, light blue eyes and chiseled features, he was already ridiculously handsome. But now those features were relaxed, his eyes smiling, and he looked almost appealing.

"Luck had nothing to do with it, or so I've been told. Great-grandma Maggie was a determined woman. She wouldn't have accepted anything less than a grandson from either one of her boys."

"Hard to believe you dislike women so much when you've got such a sterling example of womanhood as your ancestor. I doubt your great-grandmother would have approved of your attitude." He said nothing, but his mouth set in a grim line, indicating his displeasure.

Great! Maddy thought, wondering why she just didn't learn to keep her mouth shut and her opinions to herself. Of course, there were some people—CEOs of large corporations, for example—who paid a lot of money to hear those very opinions.

She'd been on the fast track with Lassiter, Owens and Cumberland until her pregnancy had caused a derailment and brought her career to a screeching halt. But she refused to think about that now. It was too depressing! Better to pull a Scarlett O'Hara and think about it later, tomorrow, never!

Hauling Maddy into the house like a sack of feed, Pete deposited her in the center of the front hallway, where they were immediately assaulted by a barking, tail-wagging mutt.

Smiling at the dog, he bent over to scratch him

behind the ear and was rewarded with several enthusiastic swipes of his tongue. "This is Rufus. He's harmless. And he likes women."

The homely creature wasn't a true Taggart then, Maddy thought uncharitably.

"Make yourself at home. Guest room's on the left at the top of the stairs. There's a bath attached and a clean robe hanging on the back of the door, if you want to take a hot soak. I'll be back in a bit. I've got to check on my animals. Make sure they're okay. Come on, Rufus." He whistled for the dog, who followed him loyally to the door, though Maddy sensed he'd rather be anywhere but outside in the cold snow.

She nodded, too startled to say much else. And what she was tempted to say could only get her into a great deal of trouble, of which she had plenty already. "Thank you," she finally managed, watching all six feet two inches of him disappear out into the frigid snowstorm.

Removing her shoes, Maddy wiggled her frozen toes, then padded across hardwood floors, inspecting first one room then another. The front parlor was filled with antique furnishings; knickknacks and framed photographs hung on rose-and-green-floral-papered walls. The Taggart family, she assumed, studying an old daguerreotype of two handsome men who looked enough alike to be brothers.

Goodness, but the Taggart men had great genes!

After making use of the bathroom, she entered the kitchen, where she found the makings for tea. Deciding to take Pete Taggart at his word, Maddy proceeded to make herself at home.

She was still cold, despite the fact the house was warmed by a very efficient woodstove. As she waited for the kettle of water to boil, she plopped down on one of the pine ladder-backed chairs at the long trestle table, which had seen some use over the years, judging from the deep scars and nicks, and surveyed the large room.

It had all the modern conveniences one would expect of a kitchen, but still retained an old-fashioned charm with the heart-of-pine cabinets and wide-planked pine flooring, covered in part by a round multicolored braided rug. Shiny copper pots hung over the center island, and cheery apple-patterned curtains framed the window over the double cast-iron sink.

The teapot whistled, and finding tea bags in one of the copper canisters on the counter, she fixed herself a cup of the steaming liquid. "Heavenly," she murmured after taking a sip, allowing the warmth to penetrate and consume her.

The back door slammed shut, and Maddy turned to find her host entering the kitchen, Rufus following close on his heels. The dog flopped down on the braided rug and promptly went to sleep.

Pete had removed his jacket and boots, but his denims were soaked from the snow; they hugged his muscular thighs in a very intriguing fashion. "I hope you don't mind," she said, not liking where her thoughts had traveled. If there was one thing she didn't need right now, it was another complication. "I made myself some tea." His face was chapped red, and he looked chilled to the bone.

"Don't mind at all, if you're sharing." He blew into his hands to warm them.

She filled a ceramic mug with hot water and a tea bag, then set it down before him. "It's a good thing you've got gas appliances, or we'd really be in a fix with the power out."

"Only the stove's gas, the rest are electric, so we're still in a fix. But I've got plenty of kerosene lanterns, and the woodstove and fireplaces will keep the house warm."

"Guess you're used to this kind of storm."

Pete shrugged, trying not to notice the way her soft brown hair, shot with streaks of gold, framed a very lovely face, or the way her eyes, the color of green clover, sparkled prettily. "I should be. I've had to live with them for thirty-six years."

"Is there a town close by? I couldn't see much of the surrounding area, with the way the snow was blowing. I need to get my car repaired."

"Sweetheart's about twelve miles to the west of us. It's small, so there aren't many amenities. If you want things like malls and movie theaters, you've got to drive to Colorado Springs or Canyon City, and I wouldn't hold your breath about the car. If Willis can tow it out, and that's a big *if*, it's doubtful he'll have the parts to make the repairs right away. He'll have to order them from Denver, and that could take a while. Plus, Willis has a real aversion to working in cold weather.''

Maddy was genuinely concerned. ''But I need my car. I need to—''

''No sense trying to buck the weather, and no use worrying over things you can't control.''

''But I don't want to be an imposition, Mr. Taggart. Is there a motel or an inn nearby where I can stay?''

Pete nodded. ''There's the Sweetheart Inn and Flannery's Motel.'' At her sigh of relief he added, ''But they're both full, because of the Christmas holidays. Looks like you're stuck with me—for now.''

''Oh, I couldn't...''

''Sweetheart's not New York City, and that's a fact, Miz Potter. I guess you'll find that out soon enough.''

Sweetheart. There was a story behind that name, she'd bet money on it. Maddy thought about all the advertising possibilities it proffered and smiled to herself.

''Sounds familiar. I grew up in a small farming community in Iowa.'' And hated every minute of it. She'd left as soon as she turned eighteen, not that her father would've noticed. Her mother had died by then, and Mary Beth had married her high school sweetheart, Lyle Randolph, so there'd been nothing to keep her there, certainly not Andrew Potter, whose only passion in life had been pigs.

She'd read once that an actress had been jealous of her famous ventriloquist father's dummy while she was growing up, which was exactly how Maddy had felt about her dad's stupid swine. He'd treated those pigs with far more affection than he'd ever shown her.

Her father was still living alone on the farm, still tending his pigs. Mary Beth kept in contact with him, but he and Maddy hadn't spoken in years. They'd never had all that much to say to each other. Nothing good, anyway.

"New York must have been quite a culture shock after Iowa," Pete remarked, drawing her attention back.

"At first, but I've grown to love it. It's got a heartbeat all its own. And you never feel alone there." Lonely, but never alone.

"I went there once with my—" He almost said *wife*, but caught himself just in time. Pete didn't like discussing Bethany with strangers, with anyone really. If Maddy noticed, she didn't let on. "Didn't much like it," he said finally.

Maddy continued sipping her tea. "Guess it's not for everyone. It's certainly not tranquil like this. How do you stand it? I'm not sure I'll be able to sleep without horns honking outside my bedroom window all night."

He studied her thoughtfully for several moments, seemed disturbed about something, then pushed back his chair and said, "If you're done, I'll show you to your room. It's got a fireplace, so you should be warm enough. Tomorrow I'll try to hook up the generator."

"I'm truly sorry to be such an imposition, Mr. Taggart. It's kind of you to put me up."

"We don't turn away stranded folks out here in the country, ma'am, so you needn't apologize. And you may as well call me Pete, seeing as how we'll be living together for an indefinite period of time."

The very idea of their "living together" was disconcerting, if not downright alarming, but she nodded anyway, following him up the stairs, thinking that it would be glorious to take off her wet stockings and soak her feet in a tub of hot water. "Where is your room located, if you don't mind my asking?"

His smile grew teasing. "Why, right next door to yours. But you needn't worry about locking your door. I think I'll be able to control myself."

Her face flamed. "I wasn't trying to imply—"

"If you need anything, just give a holler. And if you're hungry, there're sandwich makings in the cooler out on the back porch."

He walked away then, leaving Maddy to stare at the audacious man's broad back and wonder how she was going to survive in his company for even one more day, let alone an indeterminate length of time.

Chapter Two

Garbed in a green-and-white Sweetheart High School football jersey and thick woolen socks that Pete had provided for her the night before, and which were undoubtedly his, judging by the reluctant expression on his face when he'd handed them to her, Maddy made her way across the cold bedroom floor toward the bathroom.

The fire in the hearth had gone out hours before, and the ice smothering the windowpanes promised another day of snow and below-freezing temperatures.

How long was she going to have to remain stranded here? Maddy wondered. Not that she wasn't grateful for Pete Taggart's hospitality, because she was, but she needed to get to her sister's, needed to fix the mess she'd made of her life. If she could. And that was a very big *if*.

Pushing open the bathroom door, she let loose a scream. Pete Taggart was standing half-naked on the other side of it, looking like a Greek Adonis come to life. Her hand went to her throat, and her eyes widened. "Wha—what are you doing here?"

"Ouch! Dammit!" he cursed, razor in hand, turning away from the mirror over the sink to look at her startled expression. "What's it look like I'm doing? I'm shaving, that's what I'm doing." He looked quite annoyed as he blotted the bloody nick on his face with a tissue. "You might try knocking next time, instead of just barging in."

Her jaw dropped as she took in his thickly muscled chest lightly sprinkled with hair, corded biceps, and the towel that hung precariously low on his hips, which barely covered his—

"Deck the halls with boughs of holly..."

She didn't want to think about what it barely covered. Not this early in the morning.

"I—I thought this was my bathroom."

"Guess I should have made myself clearer. It's *our* bathroom. It adjoins the two bedrooms. But you're welcome to use it. When I'm not in it."

She tried to avert her gaze, but that meant she had to look into his mesmerizing blue eyes. "You might have told me that we'd be sharing this bathroom. That would have been the gentlemanly, civilized thing to do."

The sexy grin flashing across his face told her more than words that there wasn't a civilized bone in Pete Taggart's muscular, oh-so-very-fine body. "Never been accused of being civilized, *Miz* Potter, ma'am."

"You infuriate me, Mr. Taggart," she admitted,

reaching up to secure the scrunchie that had come loose during the night, and hearing him suck in his breath.

Pete's gaze zeroed in on her long, shapely legs, and his eyes filled with heat. "I wouldn't be raising your arms up like that, if I were you, ma'am, or you might be revealing more than you were intending." Not that he minded the view. It had been a long time since he'd entertained a pretty woman in his bedroom, or bathroom, for that matter.

Maddy slammed the door shut in his face, but she could still hear Pete's laughter coming through, and it filled her with outrage. Sucking in huge gulps of air, she ran to the brass cheval mirror standing in the corner and lifted her arms, observing the effect. Then she gasped.

"Good Lord!" The jersey barely covered her thighs! Why hadn't she noticed that before?

Oh no! What the man must be thinking!

WHAT THE MAN WAS THINKING was something Maddy was better off not knowing. His thoughts were X-rated, to say the least. Pete had already cursed himself many times over for finding the woman attractive. Attractive, headstrong and intelligent, despite what he'd told her. A deadly combination.

He'd sworn off women four years ago, and he didn't need this temptation, this complication in his life right now. His self-imposed celibacy—the butt of many a joke by his two younger brothers—was taking its toll. And having a half-naked woman flaunting herself at him was not helping matters in the least. Just because she hadn't intended to flaunt didn't matter. Flaunting was flaunting, no matter how you looked at it. And he sure as heck liked looking at it—her—which resulted in some pretty predictable results.

Just thinking about how she'd looked all warm and tousled from bed and dressed in his old football jersey was enough to weaken his resolve and harden his member. "Damn!" Pete fiddled with the gauges on the generator as he tried to figure out why it didn't work and cursed again.

"Why?" he asked himself. Why now when he was just getting his head back together? His heart would never mend, but he figured he could live with that.

Four years. Four years since Bethany's death, since the death of their unborn child, and the pain still festered, as if it had only been yesterday.

"I'm sorry, Pete," Dr. Reynolds had told him when he'd entered the ER that rainy afternoon four years ago. *"Bethany didn't survive the crash."*

"And the baby?"

The old man had shaken his head, and there was pity in his eyes. *"Both dead. I'm sorry, son."*

Pete blamed himself for their deaths. If he hadn't been arguing with Bethany over her new job at the radio station, if she hadn't run off half-cocked during the middle of a severe thunderstorm…

If, if, if. Too many ifs and not enough answers.

None that would suffice anyway. His wife and child were gone.

Though he took his fair share of responsibility for what had happened, he blamed Bethany more. She'd always been headstrong, bent on having her own way about working after they were married. She hadn't been content to be "just a rancher's wife" and had told him as much after they were married. She wanted to contribute, to make her mark in the world, to have it all.

The futility of what had happened angered Pete. Waste always sickened him. And Bethany's death had been a waste, and so totally unnecessary. He didn't want to think about the loss his unborn child's death had created.

His son. His child who would never see his first sunrise, kiss a girl, play baseball, go fishing with his old man.

His throat clogged, his chest ached, and he shook the painful thoughts away, though he knew they would return. They always did.

"Give it up, Taggart. It's over. Learn to live with it."

But it would never be over. Not for him.

PETE WAS NOWHERE to be found when Maddy finally mustered the courage to descend from her upstairs hideaway to the kitchen. After her humiliating encounter with him, she wanted to hide forever. But she was starving. She wasn't sure if Pete had had anything to eat, either, and so decided to take matters into her own hands and cook breakfast.

She found eggs, cheese and bacon in the cooler on the back porch, as well as a carton of orange juice. "We're saved, Rufus," she told the shaggy dog asleep on the rug. He cocked an eye open at the sound of his name, then promptly resumed his snoring.

Well, what could she expect? The dog had been living with Taggart and had no doubt picked up all his worst habits and lack of social skills.

There was hot coffee in the pot on the stove, and she poured herself a cup before scrambling the eggs. Tossing a few slices of bacon into the cast-iron skillet she found in the drawer beneath the oven, she proceeded to make culinary magic.

Maddy might not be good at reading a map or driving a car in a snowstorm, but she was an excellent cook. And she intended to prove that to the snotty, opinionated, woman-hating rancher.

"Something sure smells good," Pete said upon entering the kitchen fifteen minutes later, taking in the apron that had once belonged to his mother wrapped around Maddy Potter's waist and smiling inwardly. It wasn't quite as charming as the football jersey, but it was pretty darn cute. She'd changed back into her suit, minus the heels, and plus the woolen socks he'd loaned her.

"I wasn't sure if you'd eaten, so I decided to make us some breakfast," she explained. "I hope you don't mind."

"Don't mind at all, as long as it's edible." Being a woman didn't necessarily guarantee competency in the kitchen. Pete had learned that painful lesson shortly after he'd married. Bethany hadn't been able to boil water without burning it. She'd learned eventually, but hadn't enjoyed cooking, which resulted in her not being very good at it.

"I assure you that I cook much better than I drive, Mr. Taggart."

He snorted. "Pete."

"Only if you call me Maddy."

Pouring himself a cup of coffee, he took a sip. "Guess I can do that."

"Were you out feeding the animals?"

He shook his head. "Fed 'em at six. I was down in the basement trying to get the generator started. I've just about got it licked."

"Then we'll have electricity, right?" Most people, herself included, took modern conveniences for granted, until they went without. At the moment she would have given a great deal to be able to use her hair dryer.

Mr. Kenneth, her stylist back in New York, would have had a conniption if he'd seen Maddy's hair fashioned in something as unchic as a ponytail. Once, when she had visited his salon with her hair pulled back, he'd rudely informed her that she looked like a horse's behind. New York City stylists rarely minced words.

"As long as the gas holds out. Don't know how

much is in there, and I can't afford to siphon any out of the truck. We may need it for an emergency.''

While she continued to cook, Pete set the table and poured the juice. ''Haven't done this for a while.''

''Me, neither,'' she admitted. ''I usually just grab a bagel and cream cheese on my way to work. I rarely have time to cook anymore. And it seems silly to cook for one person anyway.''

He tilted back on the chair's hind legs. ''So, you're not married?''

She shook her head. ''No. Are you?''

''Was.'' And that was all he said, making her wonder what had happened to Mrs. Pete Taggart.

Setting the bowl of scrambled eggs and platter of sizzling hickory-smoked bacon on the table, Maddy seated herself across from him. The domesticity of the situation didn't escape her. ''I'm grateful for your hospitality, Pete. I don't know what I would have done if you hadn't happened along.''

''Probably frozen to death would be my guess.'' But he softened the words with a grin. ''Always happy to help a lady in distress.'' A pretty lady, he should have said, but knew he couldn't, or wouldn't.

''I'm happy to do my fair share around here. I don't want to be a burden. I can help with the chores, cook and clean. And I've got some money to help pay for the groceries, if you don't mind taking a check. I didn't bring much cash with me.''

''Don't need your money or your help with the animals, though I appreciate the offer. But if you want to cook, that's fine with me. That's one chore

I hate doing.'' Pete's brother was fond of saying that his beef stew tasted worse than fresh horse droppings. And John ought to know since he was Sweetheart's one and only vet.

"I—" Suddenly Maddy placed her hand over her mouth, and all color drained from her face.

"What's wrong?" Pete's eyes widened, then filled with concern at her pasty appearance. "Are you going to be sick or something?" He looked horrified at the prospect.

Not daring to answer, she nodded, then raced for the bathroom, where she promptly gave up what she'd just eaten. While she was still retching into the toilet, Pete came up behind her and handed her a damp wash cloth.

"You got the flu?"

Wiping her mouth, she faced him, feeling mortified and afraid. The concern on his face made her eyes fill with tears. "I wish it were that simple."

"Food allergies, huh? I hear they're pretty common. My mom used to be allergic to eggs."

There was no sense in lying or trying to hide the truth. Not when they had to live in the same house together. She took a deep breath. "I'm pregnant."

"Pregnant!" Paling visibly, fear entered his eyes, which he masked with anger. "You're pregnant and you were out driving in a snowstorm! How smart is that?" He turned away from her then, stalked back into the kitchen and began cursing under his breath.

Not knowing what else to do, she followed. "I'm sorry to have blurted it out like that. This is my first bout of morning sickness. I've been fine up till now.''

His fingers gripped the countertop as he stared unseeing out the window at the falling snow. When he finally got his emotions back under control he turned to face her. "I thought you said you weren't married."

Her ashen cheeks filled with color. "I'm not. It's not a prerequisite these days."

"Does your boyfriend know?"

"David's not my boyfriend. He's my boss. And he knows. He told me to have an abortion and not to come back to work until I had 'solved my little problem,' I believe was how he put it."

"You musta either been drunk-on-your-ass or crazy-in-love to have gone to bed with an ass like that."

"I was neither. And you forgot *stupid*. *Stupid* seems to be the operative word."

He glanced down at her abdomen, which was still flat as a board. He knew it wouldn't remain like that for much longer. Soon she'd be softly rounded, her breasts would enlarge, her skin would turn rosy and radiant. He remembered, all too well. "You're not very far along."

"Eight weeks. Look, Pete, I'm sorry to have dumped this on you, on top of everything else. It's my problem and I'll deal with it."

"And that's why you were going to Leadville to see your sister? To tell her about 'your problem'?"

She heaved a sigh. "Mary Beth's the only family

I've got. I haven't seen my dad in years. I—I need to talk to her, get some perspective on what I should do.'' She needed a hug and consolation, and knew she'd get both from Mary Beth. Along with a large dose of levelheadedness.

''Sounds like you've already decided not to have an abortion.''

''I couldn't. It wouldn't be fair to the baby. He or she can't help who their father is, or that their mother is an irresponsible lunatic.''

She looked so distraught that he wrapped a comforting arm about her shoulder and helped her back to the chair. Pete didn't believe in kicking a body when it was already down, and Maggie looked about as low as a person could get at the moment. Besides, who was he to moralize? He'd certainly made his fair share of mistakes.

''Sit here. I'll get you a glass of milk. That'll probably go down a lot better than the orange juice. And you should eat some dry toast. I'll fix it.''

''You can't use the toaster.''

''I'm an Eagle Scout. I'll improvise.'' And he did, using the open flame of the gas jet to toast the bread golden brown.

''Tha...thank you.'' His being nice made her want to cry, but she forced back the tears threatening to spill. She didn't think Pete Taggart was the kind of man who did well with tears and weepy women.

Placing the milk and toast in front of her, he sat down beside her. ''Eat. You'll feel better.''

''I really think I should go. I—''

"No! I'll not have another—" The wounded look in his eyes gave her pause.

He continued, "Have you looked outside? It's still snowing like crazy. You won't be going anywhere for a good long while, Maddy, so you may as well just get used to the idea that you're stuck here with me."

"But my clothes, the car..." She'd never felt so helpless. But at least she wasn't alone, and for that she was grateful.

"I'll saddle one of the draft horses and see if I can fetch your clothes. The car'll have to remain where it is, until Willis can tow it into town. Trust me. No one's going to bother it. Even a snowplow would have difficulty getting back in here now."

"Quit trying to cheer me up." She forced a strained smile.

He flicked the end of her nose and returned the smile. "I wouldn't dream of it, Miz Potter, ma'am."

This was just getting better and better, Maddy thought after he'd departed. Not only was she pregnant and unmarried, sick to her stomach and stuck out in the middle of nowhere with an arrogant rancher two weeks before Christmas, but she was starting to like Pete Taggart. And that would never do.

"I DON'T THINK *YERK* is a word. Are you sure you're not trying to cheat by making that up?"

Dressed in the jeans and blue cashmere sweater Pete had fetched from the rental car, Maddy was lying flat on her stomach in front of the parlor fireplace facing him, the Scrabble board situated between them. "Of course, it's a word. I admit, not many people use it, but it's definitely a word."

He shook his head in disbelief. "Guess I'm gonna have to challenge, then."

She smiled confidently. "Go ahead. But if you're wrong, I'm going to get the extra points, which means I'll win the game."

While Pete studied the dictionary, Maddy turned toward the fire, resting her head on her palm and staring into the blue and orange flames.

Playing Scrabble had been Pete's idea, and she was having a wonderful time beating him. Of course, she'd never before played Scrabble or any other board game by firelight and lantern light—the generator still wasn't fixed—which made the experience all that more fun and challenging.

"You win," he conceded. "Still can't believe *yerk* is a word. But it says right here—'to beat vigorously, thrash.'" He slammed the dictionary closed.

"So, how about a game of cards, say strip poker? I'm better at that."

There was a twinkle in his eye, making Maddy laugh, something she hadn't done in quite a while.

"Maybe some other time. I'm too full from dinner right now to strip."

"Those roast beef sandwiches you made were pretty good."

"And don't forget the chicken noodle soup. I'm dynamite with a can opener and water."

"What shall we do now? It's too early to go to bed." Though going to bed with Maddy Potter would be a helluva lot more stimulating than playing board games. Stimulating but not smart.

She glanced up at the tall grandfather clock ticking away in the far corner. "Eight's a bit early for me, too." She thought a moment. "Got any marshmallows? I love roasting marshmallows. And we could have some hot chocolate, if you've got any."

"Wait here," he said, launching himself to his feet, grateful to have something to take his mind off the tightening in his groin. "I can do better than that." He returned a few minutes later, carrying a large wooden tray containing a box of graham crackers, a few chocolate bars and a bag of marshmallows. "No hot chocolate, but I've got the fixings for s'mores."

"Ooh!" she said, clapping her hands. "I haven't fixed those since I was a kid."

He removed the fireplace screen and handed her a long metal skewer. My mom loved doing this, so she had my dad make her some 'marshmallow sticks,' as she called them." The memory brought a sad smile to his face. His mother had died three years ago from breast cancer. First Bethany, then his mom. All the women in his life were gone. It had been a hard burden to bear.

They sat shoulder to shoulder in companionable silence, Rufus nestled right up against Maddy's back. When Maddy bit into her first s'more she made a moan of satisfaction that went straight to Pete's lap.

"These are yummy! I think I've died and gone to heaven."

With her hair in a ponytail and an exuberant smile on her face, Maddy looked like a teenager, not a twenty-nine-year-old woman who was going to have a child. He cleared his throat. "Uh, have you been having any weird cravings lately?" he asked, trying to get his mind back on track.

She shook her head. "Not really. I eat just about everything anyway, so there's not much I crave."

"How do you feel about having this baby? Are you happy now that you've gotten used to the idea?"

She looked at him as if he'd lost his mind. "Who says I'm used to the idea? My body's still the same as it was. I'll probably feel a whole lot different when my belly grows to the size of a watermelon and my breasts—" She caught herself just in time. What on earth was she doing discussing breasts with a virtual stranger?

He grinned at her embarrassment. "You can say 'breasts,' Maddy. I'm quite familiar with those particular body parts. We ranchers have loads of experience." And she certainly had a fine pair, he couldn't help notice.

"Well, I'm not used to discussing things like this with anyone. I was so busy working that I didn't develop many close female friends. And most of the men I worked with on Madison Avenue didn't discuss female body parts as a topic of dinner conversation."

Chocolate dribbled down her chin, and he reached

over and scooped it up with his finger, then lifted it. "Stuffed shirts."

The erotic gesture made Maddy's stomach tighten, though she tried her best to ignore it. "Have you been ranching long?"

"All my life. I love it, though my two brothers don't feel the same as me. John became a vet, and Mark, who's a chef, owns a bed-and-breakfast in town called The Sweetheart Inn. The place I mentioned was full."

"A chef. Now there's a handy man to have around."

"He's divorced if you want to meet him."

Her eyes widened at the offer. "No thanks! I've pretty much sworn off men for the time being. Besides, I doubt many men would jump at the chance at meeting a pregnant woman."

"You'd be surprised. There aren't that many eligible women in town, unless you count our librarian and resident spinster Ella Grady, but she's sixty-four."

Maddy smiled before asking, "You said you'd been married. Are you divorced, too?"

He paused a moment before answering, as if considering whether he would. "Widowed. Four years now."

At the pain she saw reflected in his eyes, she reached out to touch his hand. It was obvious he was still mourning the loss of his wife. "I'm sorry. I shouldn't have pried."

He shrugged. "Time heals all wounds. Isn't that what they say?" Too bad it wasn't true.

She smiled ruefully. "Time's not going to heal what ails me. It's only going to ripen things, I fear."

"A pregnant woman's a beautiful sight to behold," he said, remembering. "And you've only got seven more months to go, then you'll have a son or daughter."

"The thought terrifies me. I don't know a thing about being a mother, raising a child. Or how I'm going to work to support it yet still be at home to care for my son or daughter. Single motherhood wasn't something they taught in college."

"Not even at Vassar?" He couldn't help his teasing smile.

"They were more into teaching prevention. Guess I was out sick that day."

"Quit being so tough on yourself, Maddy. People make mistakes. That's just part of life."

"True. But my mistake is going to be a living, breathing human being. And I'm the one who's going to be responsible for every facet of its life. It's an awesome responsibility, and one I'm not sure I can handle."

"You've got your sister. I'm sure she'll help out. That's what family's for." He wouldn't have been able to cope after Bethany's death, if it hadn't been for his brothers. John and Mark had been there for him in all the ways that counted.

"Mary Beth's always wanted a child, but she and Lyle can't conceive. I'm not sure how she's going to react to the news that I'm pregnant. It could cause problems between us."

"Have you thought about giving up the baby and allowing your sister to raise it? That would solve both her problem and yours."

Her hand moved to her abdomen, and her eyes softened. "I have, but I don't think I can give up my child, even to Mary Beth. Oh, I know she'd be a fabulous mother, and Lyle's a wonderful man. The baby would have a good home. But—" She shook her head. "It's my baby. I…I don't expect you to understand."

"But I do. Bethany was six months pregnant when she died. I lost my wife and my son in one fell swoop, so don't think I don't know what loss is, because I do. I know very well." He rose to his feet and walked out, leaving Maddy alone to sort through the mess of her life. And his.

Chapter Three

Leaning back against the goose-down pillows, Maddy shut the book she'd just finished reading and heaved a contented sigh. Pete's mother had been fond of romance novels, and there was a wicker basket full of them next to the bed.

Maddy had never considered herself the romance novel type—she'd always been fond of mysteries and science fiction. But once she'd started reading she hadn't been able to stop and had already devoured two books in less than three hours.

Too bad real life wasn't as romantic as in the novels, she thought. In romance fiction the hero loved the heroine more than life itself and married her. Happily ever after was a fait accompli. He didn't tell her to get lost and have an abortion. Of course, David Lassiter was not a hero in any way, shape or form.

Now Pete Taggart, rescuer of stranded women, was another story altogether.

Maddy smiled at the thought, feeling a wee bit guilty that Pete had spent most of the day down in the cold basement trying to fix the generator, while she had been upstairs lazing around reading books. Still, it had been heavenly to just sit back, relax and do nothing. She hadn't done something so purposely selfish in years.

The fireplace flickered softly, and Maddy ran her hand over the lovely heirloom quilt covering the bed. It had been fashioned in various colors and patterns of fabric in the wedding ring design and was exquisite. The material looked very old, and she made a mental note to ask Pete where he'd gotten it.

Maybe she could have one made for her bedroom back in New York, though it would never look as nice as it did on the antique four-poster she'd been sleeping on. There was something to be said for antiques, like real wood instead of pressboard, and brass fixtures instead of brass-plated tin.

The room where she slept was quaint and cozy compared to her white-walled bedroom back home, which now seemed stark and sterile. White had appeared so cosmopolitan when she'd first purchased her comforter and pillows. She'd painted her walls and appliances white to match the apartment's wall-to-wall carpeting. Now she wished she'd been a bit more imaginative. For a woman who made a living at being creative, her decorating skills sucked.

Gazing at the tiny yellow daffodils splayed across the walls, she smiled. You couldn't help smiling in such a room. It spoke of sunshine and happiness. The bed had been painted buttercup-yellow, as well as the dresser and nightstand, which had been stenciled in an ivy motif. Even someone with as many problems as she had at the moment couldn't help but be cheered.

"You did a good job, Mrs. Taggart," she said, caressing the quilt, unsure if she was complimenting the rancher's deceased wife or mother. "I'm not sure that praise extends to Pete—I haven't made up my mind about him yet—but your taste in decorating is just wonderful."

Suddenly the little milk-glass lamp on the bedside table flickered then lit, and Maddy's eyes widened. At first she'd thought Mrs. Taggart might be trying to reach her from the great beyond, but then realized that the clever rancher had finally fixed the generator. They had electricity!

Laughing excitedly, she hurried downstairs.

"You did it!" she said to Pete when she entered the kitchen a few moments later. He was leaning against the counter, holding a cup of coffee and looking inordinately pleased with himself. And sexy as all get-out! She stopped short of throwing herself into his arms.

He caught her huge smile and nodded. "Yep. The generator's going on a wing and a prayer, but it's going. Let's not breathe too deeply or we might jinx it."

"Oh, I can't believe it. I can finally style my hair, bake Christmas cookies—you do like cookies, don't you?"

"I—" A funny look crossed his face. Pete hadn't celebrated the holidays since Bethany's death. There didn't seem much point in giving thanks, in praising God for all he had done. God might work in mysterious ways, but Pete hadn't been able to figure out his plan in taking *his* wife and unborn child away from him.

He'd been disappointed, angry at God's handiwork. But now reflecting back on that anger, Pete realized it hadn't gotten him anywhere. It hadn't brought Bethany or the baby back. It had only served to make him miserable, lonely and embittered.

Maybe it was time to rethink things, like his brother John had urged him to do. *"You're wallowing, big brother. And miserable to be around. Get on with your life or shoot yourself in the head. I'm sick and tired of watching you go on like this."* John had never been one to mince words.

Christmas was only two weeks away. Pete knew his family, especially John, would like it if he reentered the world of the living and made an effort to attend Mark's annual Christmas party at the inn, which would be held next week.

There was a glow in Maddy's cheeks, a sparkle in her eyes, that softened Pete's heart. The woman had a lot on her plate at the moment. It wouldn't hurt to be nice, make her happy, he thought. She'd be gone soon enough, and then he'd be alone again. The idea of her leaving didn't sit very well. He'd been alone too long, and he liked having her around.

"How do you feel about Christmas trees?" he asked before he could change his mind.

"Christmas trees?" Her eyes widened at the

strange question. "Why, I love them. They smell so wonderful. Of course, I haven't had a real one in years. Last year I didn't even put one up, I was so busy working on a huge ad campaign." It suddenly occurred to Maddy that she hadn't really enjoyed Christmas in years, not since joining the prestigious advertising firm. To David Lassiter, Frank Owens and Larry Cumberland, Christmas was just another day to earn money. Sadly, she had fallen into that same trap.

"We always had a live tree when I was growing up," she added, the memory making her smile. "My mom used to make tons of popcorn and Mary Beth and I would decorate the branches with popcorn and cranberry garlands. Why do you ask?"

He shrugged, shoving his hands deeper into his pockets. "Just thought it would give us something to do tomorrow, if I was to hitch the horse to the sleigh—"

"Sleigh! You have a sleigh?" She squealed with delight, making him laugh aloud.

"Yep. It's very old and probably wouldn't make it all the way to town, but I figure if we don't go too far, we can take it and see about cutting down a tree.

"I—I haven't put one up in years myself, but since this year's kinda special..." He felt almost light-hearted at the idea, which was very odd in itself.

Special because of her? Maddy wanted to ask, unable to keep her pulse from skittering, though she knew she was being foolish. But right now, at this very moment, she just didn't care. "I'll make sand-wiches and we can have a picnic of sorts."

He arched a disbelieving brow. "In the snow?"

"You're an Eagle Scout, remember? We'll impro-vise."

AS IF THE HEAVENS approved of their plan, the snow had finally stopped falling; the sun was making a valiant effort to peek through the cloud cover. Ev-erywhere Maddy looked she saw white. From the thick frosting on the trees, to the marshmallow-covered landscape, to the frigid breath escaping her mouth.

"It's beautiful here. I can see why you wanted to keep the ranch when no one else did."

Pete turned to gaze at her, surprised by her remark. "I didn't think you liked country living." He clucked a few times and hitched the reins, urging the horse through the thick accumulation. The old sleigh's rudders glided along, slicing through the snow like a hot knife through butter.

"I don't, but I like the country. Besides, this is different country from where I grew up. We didn't have all these pretty trees and mountains. Iowa's pretty flat." Her mother used to say that if you stood at one end of the state you could see clear over to the other side.

Maddy started humming *Jingle Bells*. It seemed appropriate, considering this was her very first time to go "dashing through the snow in a one-horse open sleigh." Her enthusiasm was catching and Pete soon found himself humming the same tune, then singing out loud in a deep baritone voice. They were laughing like giddy teenagers as they finished the second verse.

"What kind of tree do you want to cut?" he asked, realizing he hadn't felt so carefree in years. It felt good. Damn good!

"A fir, natch. Is there any other kind?"

"Not to me, but I thought I'd be polite and ask anyway."

She was tempted to remark that they had a lot in common, but knew that wasn't really true. Pete was content to raise his animals and live a quiet kind of life. Maddy'd had that kind of life once before. She hadn't liked it then, and it was doubtful she'd like it now, though admittedly she found her surroundings breathtakingly beautiful. And breathing in the pure mountain air was a welcome relief from the pollution of New York City.

They spotted a stand of fir trees a short distance ahead, and Maddy pointed enthusiastically. "There's the one we should get. Do you see it? That big one over there, next to the decaying tree stump."

Pete's gaze rose up and up, and his eyes widened as he pulled the sleigh to a halt. "Are you crazy? That tree's too tall. It'll never fit in the family room. The ceilings are only twelve feet high."

"But you could trim just a bit off the top and bottom, couldn't you? I could help."

He rubbed his chin, considering. "I doubt if I have enough lights and ornaments for such a huge tree,

Maddy." And there was also the problem of dragging it home. He doubted the old sleigh could take the strain.

She gazed imploringly at him. "But we could—"

"Improvise," he finished with a wry grin. "Got it."

"Oh, look—mistletoe! We'll need some to hang in the doorway." Then noting his odd look, she blushed, embarrassed by what he must be thinking. "I'm sorry. I guess we don't—"

"We should have mistletoe," he agreed. "It's traditional, right?" And one never knew when it would come in handy.

Watch it, Taggart! You're heading down a dangerous path.

But Pete couldn't seem to help himself. It was like some strange spell had been cast on him and he was powerless to resist.

Maddy, the Madison Avenue witch, was proving downright intoxicating.

"I TOLD YOU IT WOULDN'T fit."

Gazing at the huge tree, which took up half of the family room, Maddy's eyes lit with appreciation. They'd had to move most of the furniture to the other side to accommodate it, but the effort had been worth it. "It's beautiful." She smiled happily. "Just perfect. And once it's decorated it's going to look even better."

Pete looked skeptical. As he'd suspected, the Douglas Fir was much too big for the room. And it was a big room! "I can see you're not the kind of woman to give up on an idea once you put your mind to it."

She crossed her arms over her chest and arched a brow. "How do you think I became successful in a male-dominated profession?"

"I'll need to trim a bit more off the top, if we're going to put the angel up there. Then I can start hanging the lights."

"While you're doing that, I'll go and bake us some cookies. If it's okay to use the oven, that is. I hope so, because you can't have a tree-trimming party without cookies."

"Might as well go ahead. And having cookies to eat will make the chore of decorating the tree somewhat palatable." And he knew John would most likely bring extra gas when he came over to check up on him. His younger brother was worse than a mother hen.

"It'll be fun. You'll see."

He shook his head. "I thought pregnant women were supposed to be tired all the time. You seem to be bursting with energy."

"I refuse to let this pregnancy slow me down. Having a baby's as natural as breathing, right?" She'd mentally challenged herself not to have any more bouts of morning sickness. So far she'd been successful. "I bet your great-grandma Maggie was out plowing fields right after she birthed those big strapping sons of hers."

"Maybe branding cows. But Maggie would never

have pushed a plow. The woman was a rancher, not a farmer.''

''Whatever,'' Maddy said, not caring much about the distinction as she sailed out of the room.

City girl, he reminded himself. And would keep reminding himself whenever he started getting stupid ideas. He'd been having a lot of stupid ideas lately where Maddy was concerned.

He and Maddy Potter were about as different as any two people could be. He'd be wise to remember that fact.

Pete was up to his ears in lights and tree branches when Maddy floated back into the room an hour later, carrying a large tray laden with coffee and cookies. ''Time for a break, Santa. I've brought treats.''

He descended the tall ladder, looking disheveled and twice as frustrated. ''We've only got enough lights for the top half of the tree. It's gonna look ugly. I tried to—''

She held a cookie out to him. The sweet smell of vanilla wafted up, and he inhaled deeply before taking it. ''It's going to be perfectly lovely. Once we get on the decorations you're not going to notice how many lights there are. Besides, we're not entering a contest. We're merely doing this for our own enjoyment. Are you this much of a perfectionist about everything?''

He bit into his cookie and plopped down onto the sofa next to her. ''Mmm. These are good.'' A fire was blazing in the large stone fireplace. His parents had added the large family room three years before his dad's death, and it was his favorite room in the old house. The bank of windows at the rear allowed in plenty of light, affording a magnificent view of the gently rolling landscape and mountains beyond.

"Yep. Can't stand not being the best at everything. Just ask my brothers. It drives them nuts." He seemed pleased by that notion and reached for a handful of cookies.

"I'd be happy to ask your brothers. When do you think I'll get to meet them?" She hoped soon, because she doubted she'd be around too much longer. The thought saddened her.

Get real, Maddy! You've already made one huge mistake. Don't compound it by making another. Pete Taggart's got more baggage than Grand Central Station. And so do you, for that matter!

"I suspect now that the snow's let up John'll be making his way over to check up on me. He's the worrywart of the family, too conscientious for his own good. He has a snowmobile, so he can get around better than most."

"And is this adventurous, worrywart-of-a-brother of yours married?"

"Nope. John's still a bachelor. Don't think he dates that much. All of his passion's been poured into his animals and veterinary clinic. He's a fine vet. Sweetheart's lucky to have him."

"So all three of the Taggart men are single? And the only eligible woman for miles around is the spinster librarian? Does that about sum it up?"

He grinned sheepishly. "Something like that, though there might be a single woman or two in town. Just no one that appeals to any of us." That wasn't quite true. John was still hung up on Allison Montgomery, though the woman didn't seem to feel the same way about him.

"I guess I'm not surprised, then, that you're all still unmarried, as picky as you seem to be."

"Well, you're pretty choosy yourself. I don't see you married and settled down yet, either."

Her face flushed. "Apparently I wasn't choosy enough. I didn't date all that much, and I guess I was flattered by the amount of attention an older, successful man paid to me. I guess he was only after one thing, but I was too stupid and naive to realize it."

He'd meant to tease, not hurt her. "Someday you'll meet someone. You seem the type of woman to be married."

Pete's comment annoyed the heck out of Maddy, and she stiffened. "Why, because I bake cookies and decorate Christmas trees? That's a rather old-fashioned assumption, Pete Taggart, if you don't mind my saying so. A modern woman can do a lot of—"

He held up his hand. "Please, spare me the 'I am woman, hear me roar' speech. I've heard it before."

There was pain in his eyes, and she was sure he was thinking about his dead wife, but Maddy didn't press. It was none of her business anyway. "Since it's obvious we don't see eye to eye on women in the workplace, why don't we continue on with decorating the tree? Where are the ornaments? I'll fetch them.''

He felt stupid and small for picking a fight with her. Maddy was a successful career woman with a life back in New York. What did it matter if her goals were different from his? He barely knew the woman. And yet, he felt as if they'd known each other all their lives. It was strange how quickly they'd connected. Strange and worrisome.

''The ornaments and such are kept in the storage closet in the guest room. I'll carry them down for you. You shouldn't be lifting things in your condition.''

She brushed off his concern with a wave of her hand. ''Don't be silly. You've got enough to contend with at the moment. I might look like a weakling, but I'm strong as an ox. Being pregnant doesn't change that.'' She lifted her arm. ''Feel my muscle. I work out with weights.''

Smiling inwardly, he wrapped his hand around the puny biceps and squeezed gently. ''You sure you've been working out?''

She made a face, then said, ''By the way—you know that lovely wedding ring quilt that's covering the bed in the guest room? Do you have any idea where it came from? I'd like to have one made just like it for my apartment in New York.''

''It was my mother's. She left it to me, as the oldest Taggart, in her will when she died. Mom inherited it from her mother. The quilt originally belonged to Great-Grandma Maggie and has been passed down from generation to generation.

"The old trunk it originally came in sits in the far corner of the guest room, next to the rocker. You can look and see if there's a pattern or something in there you can use to make one."

Maddy laughed, as if the idea was totally absurd. "I'm not that clever. Cooking and thinking up brilliant ad campaigns are about as creative as I get. Sewing is not one of my talents. Now Mary Beth, she can sew just about anything. I intend to talk her into making me a replica of the quilt."

Pete didn't doubt for a moment that she could. Maddy Potter could sweet-talk anyone into doing just about anything. He gazed at the too-tall tree and sighed.

A sweet-talking woman was trouble. A sweet-talking, pretty woman—well, a smart man would run for cover and hide.

Pete had always credited himself with being smart. Until now.

MADDY WAS WAVING an old wrinkled piece of parchment when she reentered the family room a short time later. She looked so enthralled with whatever she held that Pete's curiosity sparked immediately, and he set aside the sports magazine he was reading.

"All right, I'll bite. What did you find, a pattern for the quilt?"

Her eyes were wide with wonder when she said, "You're not going to believe this, Pete." She plopped down on the sofa and leaned toward him. "This paper was in the trunk, hidden beneath tissue-wrapped baby clothes. I hope you don't mind. I just couldn't resist looking at those tiny garments." Seeing those clothes had made her pregnancy seem all too real.

Maddy smelled like vanilla and cinnamon, and Pete's heart started pounding. He was hungry, but not for cookies, and took a deep breath. "I don't mind. Now, are you going to tell me what that paper says?" He couldn't recall ever seeing it before, but then he hadn't felt much like going through his mother's possessions after she died. It would have been too painful. Sorting through Beth's things had been difficult enough.

"It's a legend about the wedding ring quilt, and it looks to be quite old. Listen to this—'Place this quilt upon your bed and in one month you shall be wed, but if you think you'd rather not, then a spinster's life shall be your lot.' Isn't that something?"

Pete paled somewhat. A legend about the quilt that foretold of a wedding? It couldn't be true, could it? "It's probably just something my great-grandmother made up."

"Maybe. But I also found a letter written to one of her sons. Apparently Maggie wanted him to marry, settle down and have children, so the ranch would pass on to a Taggart. And she didn't mince words. From the stern tone of the letter, I think her son, Jared, was pretty resistant to the idea."

"Taggart men don't like being told what to do."

"Well, since you're here as living proof, I guess

your great-grandmother got her way, because it's obvious both her sons eventually married and had children—your ancestors.''

Pete digested what she'd said then flashed a teasing grin. ''Well, Maddy, if you truly believe in the legend then you might just find yourself in the same predicament as my great-uncles.''

Her brow wrinkled in confusion. ''What do you mean?''

''You've been sleeping under the wedding ring quilt for a couple of nights now. If the legend's true, and you seem to think it is, you'll be married before a month is up.''

She reread the legend and gasped. Then realizing that there were actually two pages of paper not just one, she ran her thumbnail between the sheets and unstuck them, reading to herself. ''A man and a woman who meet if by chance, will soon be doing the marital dance. A kiss on the lips, the bargain will seal, and undying love will the couple soon feel.''

''Good heavens! This can't be true.'' She forced a nervous laugh. ''You're right. It was just something your great-grandma Maggie made up.'' She and Pete hadn't kissed. They had nothing to worry about.

''What is it? What's it say?'' He tried to grab the paper from her hand, but she held it behind her back and out of his reach.

''Nothing.'' She shook her head. ''It's nothing. Really. Just fanciful musings of an elderly woman, I'm sure.''

''I don't believe you. You turned as pale as that

snow outside the window when you read it. Now let me see what it says.''

Maddy tried to scoot away, but Pete grabbed her gently about the waist and pinned her down with his body, being careful not to crush her with his weight.

Pete was no longer interested in wrestling for the paper, not when Maddy's lips were mere inches away and he had a burning desire to kiss her.

Licking his lips in anticipation, his intention reflected quite clearly in his eyes, Maddy panicked. ''Pete, wait! Don't do it! You don't under—''

''I'm sorry, Maddy, but I've got to.'' He covered her mouth with his own, cutting off her protest, and plundered the honey within, savoring the sweet, irresistible taste of her. Like a starving man he feasted, unable to get his fill.

Losing herself in the passion of the moment, Maddy allowed him to taste, tease and nibble. Until she remembered the words written on the paper, and then she panicked.

Pushing hard against the granite wall of his chest, she was finally able to break free of his hold. ''Stop, Pete! You've done a terrible thing!''

He was breathing hard, his eyes heavy lidded with passion, but he didn't look at all contrite. ''Oh, come on now, Maddy,'' he finally said. ''It was only a kiss. I'm sorry if you're offended, but I just couldn't help myself.''

''I know that. It's because of this.'' She reached behind her, grasped the paper and thrust it at him.

''You've just sealed our fate with that kiss, Pete Taggart. So what are you going to do about it?''

Chapter Four

His face solemn, Pete finished reading the paper and handed it back to Maddy. "Well, I guess there's only one thing left to do—I'll have to marry you."

Her eyes widened, and her mouth gaped open, then she said, "Marry me? Are you crazy? We hardly know each other." The idea was ridiculous, totally absurd, yet somewhere in her heart of hearts it sounded so appealing. But then noting the twinkle in his eyes, the twitch at the corners of his mouth, she knew he'd only been teasing and felt slightly bereft.

Pete threw back his head and laughed. "Do you really think this is more than just nonsense? Come on, Maddy. It's an old woman's scribbling. Maggie was probably senile or something when she wrote it."

"From what you've told me of your great-grandmother, she didn't sound the least bit senile to me. I'd say the woman was pretty darn shrewd. And yes, I do think it's true." She didn't know why she thought that. She just did. Call it women's intuition or a gut feeling, but deep down inside she knew that the legend of the wedding ring quilt was as real as the smirk on the rancher's face that said he didn't share her beliefs.

"Are you sure it's not just your present circumstances making you want to believe? After all, being pregnant and unmarried does carry a certain stigma, even in this day and age."

She stiffened, drawing herself up to her full five feet six inches. "How dare you insinuate that I'm looking for a husband! That couldn't be further from the truth. And don't flatter yourself, Mr. Taggart. Even if I was, I wouldn't be dangling my line in your pond."

He'd wounded her pride, and for that he was sorry. But damn! This whole scenario was making him nervous. Especially after realizing that marriage to Maddy wouldn't be all that bad. Very dangerous thinking on his part.

"Now, Maddy, don't go getting all upset. It's not good for you or the baby. I'm sorry. I just thought—"

"That I was some desperate, pathetic creature? Well, I can assure you I'm not. I don't need a husband to raise this baby. I am perfectly capable of doing it on my own."

"That's not what you were saying the other night. I just thought—"

"Well, I've changed my mind. A woman can do that, you know. Change her mind, that is."

She looked so self-righteous and outraged that he wanted to pull her into his arms and kiss her senseless again. But he didn't think she'd appreciate that. Not at the moment. "I guess since you're mad at me this wouldn't be the best time to invite you to a Christmas party, huh?"

"A Christmas party?" Her annoyance was replaced quickly by confusion. "Are you insane?" She glanced toward the window, then back at him. "We're still snowed in here, or hadn't you noticed?"

"I noticed, but I think the roads might improve some by next week. We've already had a bit of melting. And if not, we'll borrow John's snowmobile or try to take the sleigh."

Curiosity got the better of Maddy, and the fact that she loved parties and rarely got to attend any, unless they were boring business functions—cocktail parties with snooty clients. "Whose party is it?" she asked, wanting to know though she had no intention of accepting the invitation, not after the insulting things he implied, even if there was a tiny kernel of truth mixed in. Plus, she needed to think about leaving. She had obviously overstayed her time here; it was definitely time to go. How she would accomplish that, she had no idea.

"My brother Mark holds a Christmas party every year at the inn. I haven't been in years, and I was thinking about going. Thought you might like to go with me."

Her heart was thundering so loudly in her chest, she was sure he could hear it. But she wouldn't give him the satisfaction of knowing how thrilled she was that he'd asked. And so she said, "Are you sure you want to risk being seen in public with a pregnant woman? After all, people might talk. They might think I'm trying to snare you into marriage against your will by conjuring up an ancient quilt legend."

He smiled ruefully. "Okay, I deserved that. Now let's have a truce, okay? I said I was sorry. And I don't much care what anyone thinks. I live my life to suit myself."

"And if I accept, you won't accuse me of having ulterior motives?"

He held up three fingers. "Scout's honor."

Pete Taggart's boyish charm could have melted ice off a glacier in subzero weather, and Maddy wondered how safe her heart was from this impossible man. Not very, she'd wager.

He'd been kind to her, and more than generous with his home and time, and she didn't want to repay him by appearing small and churlish in refusing the invitation. And she'd be gone as soon as her car got fixed. Gone away from his engaging smile, tempting kisses and brooding good looks.

At least that's what she told herself when she finally accepted.

"WELL NOW, I WASN'T expecting to find Pete entertaining a pretty woman during the middle of a blizzard. No wonder we haven't heard from him."

Gasping aloud, Maddy spun on her heel and nearly dropped the bowl of mashed potatoes she held in her shaking hands as she confronted the intruder. The man looked like a younger version of Pete, and she knew instantly that he was John, his brother. His very handsome brother.

"'Hark the herald angels sing…'"

"What was that, ma'am?"

Her face crimsoned. "Nothing. You scared me half to death!"

He removed his hat and looked suitably chastised. "I'm sorry, ma'am. I shouldn't have sneaked up on you like that. Pete's my brother. I usually just walk in. I'm John Taggart." He held out his hand, then realizing he still had on his gloves, removed them.

Maddy set down the bowl of potatoes and took his hand, which felt as cold as a frozen margarita. Lately she'd been having a craving for margaritas, though she knew alcohol wasn't particularly good for pregnant women. "I've been expecting you, Mr. Taggart. Pete said it was likely you'd be stopping by soon."

He grinned, displaying even white teeth and two dimples in his cheeks. "Oh he did, did he?" John sniffed the air like a bloodhound. "Something sure smells good. Is that ham I smell frying in the pan?"

"You've got a good nose, Mr. Taggart, and you're more than welcome to stay for dinner."

"John. And don't mind if I do. A man gets sick of his own cooking, and that's a fact."

"Okay. John." She smiled. "Just don't go sneaking up on me again, and we'll get along fine."

"Where's that brother of mine? Don't tell me he's gone off and left you stranded out here all alone?"

She couldn't tell if he was teasing or not. Taggart men liked to tease, she'd discovered. "Pete's feeding the animals. He should be back any moment."

The tall man pulled out a chair and straddled it, leaning his arms over the back. "I don't believe you said what it was you were doing here, ma'am, if you don't mind my asking. My brother didn't mention that he was expecting any out-of-town guests."

Remembering Pete's comments about his brother's overprotectiveness, and knowing her sister was of a similar mind set, Maddy smiled inwardly and explained the circumstances of her visit. "Your brother's been just wonderful about putting me up, John, but I really think it's time for me to go. Now that the storm's abated somewhat and the roads are a bit better—"

"Who said they're better?" Pete asked upon entering, nodding perfunctorily at his brother, who was grinning like a fool, and flashing Maddy an impatient look. "They're not *that* much better, and you're not going anywhere, woman. Besides, Willis hasn't picked up the car yet."

Maddy sat back in her chair, and her eyes narrowed imperceptibly. The man was impossibly hardheaded, and liked giving orders and having them obeyed. She knew Pete had her best interests at heart, but she didn't like anyone telling her what to do, especially the arrogant rancher. She was a grown woman used to taking care of herself, for heaven's sake! And she'd been doing just fine on her own before Pete Taggart had come along.

"Let's be realistic, Pete. I can't stay here forever. The rental company is going to want their car back."

"Well, big brother," John said, a twinkle in his blue eyes, which were a shade darker than his brother's. "Aren't you just full of surprises?"

Pete ignored her protest. "I see you met my brother, Maddy. Hope John hasn't been giving you a bad time. He's known for that."

No more than you, she wanted to say but refrained. "Well, he did take ten years off my life when he arrived unannounced, but other than that, no. I invited John to stay for dinner. Hope that's okay."

"It is, as long as Dr. Taggart's brought some gas for my generator."

The handsome vet grinned, and Maddy sucked in her breath. She was beginning to wonder if all of the single women living in Sweetheart were insane. Or blind. How could any normal, heterosexual woman allow the three Taggart brothers to remain unattached? Of course, looks weren't everything, she reminded herself. Their temperaments probably had something to do with their marital status.

"It's tied to the back of my snowmobile. I figured you'd be running low long about now. Brought some food, too. Didn't know you had such a lovely woman cooking for you."

Pete didn't like the admiring way John was looking at Maddy, and he had half a mind to rescind the dinner invitation. The hell of it was she didn't seem to mind the man's attention at all.

Women were fickle creatures. Not that he cared. Much.

Placing the remaining dishes of green beans, ham and biscuits on the table, Maddy set another place for Pete's brother. "Dinner's ready," she announced, and Pete sat down across from her. John came around the table to hold out her chair, and she flashed him a grateful smile. "Thank you. I'm not used to such polite treatment from a Taggart."

Pete's look grew thunderous, and the tall man threw back his head and laughed. "No one's ever accused my big brother of being polite, Maddy. He's been living out here alone for too long. Folks in town think he's a hermit. They call him the Howard Hughes of Sweetheart behind his back."

"I'd appreciate it if you two didn't talk about me as if I wasn't here. And Maddy's already been warned that I don't have many civilized traits."

Remembering the bathroom incident when she'd first arrived, Maddy's cheeks filled with color, and she prayed silently that Pete wasn't going to elaborate.

"This lovely lady here tells me that you rescued her during the height of the blizzard," John said to his brother. "Bet she was glad you came along when you did."

Maddy reached for a biscuit and slathered it with butter and honey. Lately her appetite had grown enormous. She'd be as big as one of Pete's cows soon if she didn't get it under control.

"I'm very grateful for Pete's help and hospitality,

John. Your brother might not hold out my chair, but he's been a gracious host under very difficult circumstances.''

"You don't say? That doesn't sound like my brother at all.''

"Shut up, John, and eat your ham, before I kick your butt outta my house.'' Pete turned his attention to Maddy and her previous comment about leaving.

"The roads might be getting a bit better, but they're not good enough for you to be thinking about driving off. Not to mention that your car's busted all to hell. Besides, you said you'd go to Mark's party with me, and you can't back out now. Not after you promised.''

John's brow shot up as he studied the couple. Maddy's cheeks were flushed softly, her eyes filled with tenderness as she gazed at his brother. Pete had that smitten arrow-through-the-heart look that was a sure sign he'd fallen hard for the pretty young woman. John knew enough about animal instinct to know something was in the air. Something good. Pete had been alone far too long.

"Hey, that's great news! Don't know how you managed to bring Pete out of his shell, Maddy, but my brother Mark and I are mighty grateful. No one's been able to talk him into attending the annual Christmas party for years. Or any other social function, for that matter.''

Maddy felt her cheeks warm. "I—'' She wasn't about to confess her feelings on the subject, or kid herself, for that matter. She was positive it was the quilt legend that had brought about Pete's change of heart, not anything having to do with her.

"Maddy doesn't harangue me the way you and Mark do," Pete informed his brother. "And I told you I'd come when I was damn good and ready."

The tension in the room grew palpable as the two men stared daggers at each other. Maddy sought to ease it by changing the subject. "How are things in town? Are the phone lines still out?" she asked John.

"The electricity and phones have been restored for two days now, but I'm afraid the outlying regions won't have theirs turned back on for a while yet. The damage to the power and phone lines was extensive, as you've learned firsthand."

Pete flashed her an I-told-you-so look. "Maddy was on her way to visit her sister in Leadville when she got caught in the storm."

"For the holidays?" The younger Taggart reached for another slice of ham and a biscuit. "It's nice to be with family for the holidays." He stared pointedly at his brother.

Hesitating, Maddy gazed at Pete, noting his shrug that said he was leaving any explanation about her pregnancy up to her. "Uh. Yes, it is. My sister Mary Beth and I are very close."

"Mighty tasty ham, Maddy. It'd almost be worth getting married to be able to eat like this every night."

Thanking him, she said, "I'm curious, John. Why are you so against marriage?"

The man got a peculiar look on his face. "I'm not, really. Just saving myself for the right woman."

Snorting in disbelief, Pete shook his head. "You know damn well, John David, that Allison Montgomery is never going to marry you. My brother's been pining after the same woman since high school," he explained to Maddy. "Trouble is, she thinks of him as a friend and not as husband material."

"I've always thought that the best relationships, the most successful marriages, are the ones based on friendship," Maddy offered, hoping to ease the pain she saw reflected in John's eyes. "Without friendship and mutual respect, there's no point in the rest."

The vet held up his glass of water. "Hear, hear. Finally words of intelligence, and from a pretty woman, no less. You could take lessons, brother."

Pete watched the interplay between Maddy and his brother, and he felt like breaking something, mostly John's neck. The woman was smiling prettily, staring all dreamy-eyed at his too-handsome brother, and that didn't set well, not well at all.

"YOUR BROTHER'S VERY NICE," Maddy said to Pete an hour later while washing the dishes, handing the rancher a platter to dry.

John had left immediately after dinner and gone back to his animal hospital to check on Willis Helmsley's golden retriever, who'd broken his leg earlier that day after slipping on an icy step. Willis was always doing everyone favors, so John didn't feel he could refuse him one in return. He'd promised to pass along Maddy's message to Willis about getting her car fixed.

"Hard to be objective about someone who used to put poison oak leaves in my underwear drawer," Pete said.

Glancing over her shoulder at the man's annoyed expression, Maddy burst out laughing. "Mary Beth and I used to play terrible tricks on each other, too. Once, when I was in ninth grade and she was a junior in high school, I cut all the feet out of her panty hose. She was furious, because my mom made her wear socks to school with her flats."

"And that's bad?"

Steam was rising from the water, making Maddy's cheeks rosy. "Very bad. Only geeks wore socks with their flats. That'd be like a boy wearing hard-soled shoes and white socks with shorts."

"I wonder if Mark knows he's a geek?" Pete grinned, and she slapped him playfully on the arm with the dishrag.

"Well, you'd better not tell him what I said, Pete Taggart, or I won't go to the party with you."

Placing his hands on either side of her, he effectively trapped her against the counter. "Is that so? And who would you rather go to the party with— my brother John?"

She took a moment to consider. "Your brother's very handsome," she admitted. "And he has nice manners."

He pressed closer. "Careful, woman, or you might find yourself seated in that sinkful of soapy water."

Laughter bubbled up her throat. "I sense some competitiveness between you and your younger brother."

"Always. That's the nature of siblings." He leaned closer and nibbled her ear. "You sure do smell good, Maddy." He licked the sworl and nibbled the lobe. "I bet you taste even better."

Gooseflesh erupted over her arms, and her knees grew weak with longing. Then, remembering the legend and what it foretold, she pushed at him to put distance between them. "You'd better stop that, Pete. I know it's just the legend having an effect on you, but—"

Taking a step back, he stared at her as if she'd lost her mind. "You make me hot, Maddy Potter. Hot and hard. I haven't felt this way about a woman in a very long time, and it doesn't have a damn thing to do with that stupid piece of paper you found.

"Why's it so hard for you to believe that I'm attracted to you, that your scent drives me nuts, that looking at your delectable bottom in a tight pair of jeans is enough to send me over the edge? I haven't felt this randy since I was in high school."

Her eyes widened. "I—" She swallowed. "We hardly know each other, and—"

He pulled her to his chest and kissed her, hard at first, plunging his tongue into her mouth, until he heard her moan, then softening the strokes, grazing her teeth, sucking her lower lip, pressing his hands flat against her buttocks and pulling her in to feel the hardness of his erection.

"There're certain parts of me, babe, that think we've known each other long enough." He stared intently into green eyes gone dark with passion. "You want me. I know you do. Why don't you admit it?"

Taking his hand, she placed it on her abdomen. "Because raging hormones and poor judgment got me into trouble once before. I won't allow myself to fall into that trap again."

He unsnapped her jeans, and she gasped, clutching his hand. "Stop! I can't!" But she wanted to. Oh, how she wanted to.

"I'm not going to do anything you don't want me to, Maddy. I promise. Trust me."

How can I? When I can't trust myself?

Pulling the zipper down, he placed his hand on the naked flesh resting above her underpants. "I just want to feel the baby. It's a miracle that a tiny being is growing inside you right now." He dropped to his knees and pressed kisses to her warm flesh, and Maddy thought she would lose it right there on the kitchen floor.

He was so gentle, so worshipful, that it made her heart ache. She caressed his soft hair. "I'm sorry you lost your child, Pete. I can only imagine how difficult it must have been for you."

"It was," he said hoarsely, rising to his feet. "I've always wanted a child. I—" Without another word, he grabbed his coat and slammed out the back door.

Tears filled Maddy's eyes. "Oh, Pete, if only

things had been different, for both of us." She placed her hands where his had recently been and heaved a deep sigh of longing.

"If only things were different," she whispered.

Anne Cousin

for her place, he had quickly been undone by a
deep sigh of longing.

"If only things were different," she whispered.

Chapter Five

The Sweetheart Inn was a majestic old Victorian mansion that had stood on the corner of Willow and Main streets for over a century.

Hundreds of tiny white lights decorated the roof gables and outlined the many windows and massive front doors of the three-story mansion. The large oaks and maples, now denuded of leaves, had also been strung with Christmas decorations, as had the enormous holly bushes flanking the wide front porch.

The entire effect, as it reflected off the snow-covered ground was breathtakingly beautiful. Like a child on Christmas morning, Maddy stared wide-eyed and mouth agape. "It's wonderful!" she finally declared. "I've never seen anything so magical. Even the decorated windows in New York can't compare."

Look in the mirror, Pete wanted to say, because Maddy's face shone far more brilliantly and beautiful than any Christmas light or decoration. Miraculously the sleigh still functioned. Pulling the horse-drawn vehicle to a halt, he replied, "Mark goes all out every year. He does it mostly for his kids, I think." Though Pete suspected that there was a lot of "little kid" still left in his youngest brother.

"I feel so underdressed in this skirt and sweater, especially since you look so *GQ* in your dark blue suit. Are you sure I look all right?" The green wool skirt and ornamental Christmas sweater were the only suitable garments she'd found in her suitcase to wear. She hadn't thought it necessary to pack any of her cocktail dresses when she'd left New York, but now wished she had.

She wanted to look pretty for Pete, though Maddy refused to question herself as to why, fearing what the answer might be. The longer she stayed, and the more time she spent in his company, the more attached she became to the rancher.

"Well, you'd probably look a sight better naked, I'd wager, but I think the Christmas sweater is just the right touch." He gazed at her breasts hidden by the raincoat and envied the Santa Claus emblazoned there. "Santa's never looked so good," he said, eyes twinkling.

"You're awful, Pete Taggart." Maddy shook her head and flashed him an exasperated look, and the tiny bells on the front of her sweater tinkled. "I'm not sure I should have come tonight. You promised to be on your best behavior."

He held out his hands in supplication, looking as innocent as a newborn babe. "Hey, this *is* my best behavior." Clasping her arm, he said, "Come on. I want you to meet my niece and nephew before the rest of the crowd arrives.'' And he wanted to introduce Maddy to Mark before the obsessive chef-turned-innkeeper became absorbed in the party.

A huge fir tree greeted them as they stepped into the front hallway of the mansion. It was decorated with red and silver cupids and hearts, some store-bought, others handmade by the children, and Maddy found herself looking forward to the day when she could do creative projects with her own children.

''Hey, squirt!'' Pete said to the little girl with the long blond braids who ran up to greet them. Dressed in a red velvet gown trimmed with ecru lace and black patent-leather shoes, she looked adorable. ''How's my sweet Sarah doing? Got a kiss for your old Uncle Pete?''

The child obliged by wrapping her small arms around her uncle's neck and bussing him noisily on the lips, making Maddy's heart twinge. Soon after, a pint-size boy of about four came bounding in like a playful puppy. As soon as he spotted his uncle, he made a mad dash for the rancher's long legs, entwining himself around them like an ivy vine.

''Uncle Pete! Uncle Pete! Carry me on your shoulder, Uncle Pete. *Pleeeze!*''

''And muss up your nice suit? I don't think so, sport.'' Pete ruffled the child's hair. ''Your dad would have my hide.''

Taking the children by the hand, Pete brought them over to meet Maddy. ''This is my houseguest, Maddy Potter. She's one of your guests for the evening, so be extra special nice to her. "These two rug-rats are my niece, Sarah, and nephew, Evan."

Smiling in greeting at the suddenly shy duo, Maddy was about to comment on how nice they looked when the little girl blurted, "Is she your sweetheart, Uncle Pete?" Sarah crossed her arms over her chest in a very grown-up fashion and looked very put out, as only a six-year-old child could. "'Cause you told me I was your sweetheart. And it's not nice to lie, my daddy said so."

Eyes filled with tenderness, Pete opened his arms and the little girl rushed into them. "Maddy's a good friend. And though she's pretty sweet—" he gave Maddy a wink "—you'll always be my special girl, Sarah."

The child's face was effused with pleasure, and Maddy knew then and there that Pete Taggart was a silver-tongued devil who could charm the socks off a centipede.

Maddy also knew that she was doomed, because, unless she was very much mistaken, she was falling in love with the handsome rancher.

"Well, I can hardly believe my eyes." A dark-haired man with the trademark Taggart blue eyes strolled in. He was dressed in a white chef's jacket and gray checked pants, and while not quite as tall as his brothers, he was just as handsome. Well, maybe not quite as handsome as Pete, but pretty darn close. Though he was the youngest of the three, Mark Taggart's temples were already starting to silver, giving him a distinguished appearance.

The innkeeper's grin was engaging as he pumped his brother's hand, then he grabbed Pete by the arm and pulled him in for a hug. "Glad you could come, brother. We've missed your ugly mug around here."

Heat crept up the rancher's face to land squarely on his cheeks. "Mark, I'd like you to meet Maddy Potter. She's been staying with me during the storm."

A dark brow shot up and mischief twinkled in his eyes. "Is that so?" Mark flashed a knowing smile. "John's told me a little bit about that."

At Pete's look of annoyance, Maddy, fearing the worst, thought it wise to butt in. "Your inn's lovely, Mark. Pete's told me a little bit about your efforts to restore this old house. You've done a wonderful job."

From the warm patina of the dark walnut paneling and moldings, to the sparkling crystals on the chandeliers overhead and colorful Aubusson rugs on the oak parquet floor, Maddy knew that a lot of love and hard work had gone into refurbishing the wonderful old house. Even Bob Vila would have been impressed. She certainly was.

"Thanks. I've poured a lot of sweat and money into this drafty old relic. More of the latter, I'm afraid. Now I just hope my investment pays off. Aside from the Christmas holiday, business has been slow, and I don't know what to do about it."

Maddy's brows rose in surprise. "Really? I find that hard to believe. As lovely as everything is, you should be fighting off the customers."

"Yeah, that's what I thought, too. I mean—everyone who stays here seems to enjoy the experience. And I know the food is good." His confident grin brought a snort from his brother. Lack of self-confidence was not a Taggart trait.

"Have you been advertising in the right areas, using the Internet to get the word out? That's my area of expertise, and I'd be happy to sit down with you and make some suggestions for the inn, keeping in mind your overall advertising objectives, if you'd like." Her mind started formulating all sorts of possibilities about sweetheart weekends, balls and the like, and she smiled enthusiastically. Maddy was always up for a challenge.

Ignoring Pete totally, Mark's face lit with a smile as he wrapped his arm about Maddy's shoulders and led her into the front room, where another magnificent tree resided, this time decorated in an antique Santa theme of red and gold. Pete trailed behind the couple, looking glum and very annoyed.

"So, Maddy, John tells me you're still unattached. Are all the men in New York City blind and stupid?" Mark asked. The vein in Pete's temple started throbbing when Maddy, *his* date for the evening, laughed gaily and strolled off on the arm of his brother, ignoring him completely.

"YOU MUST BE MADDY POTTER," the attractive blonde said as she approached a short time later, holding out a cup of eggnog to her. "John told me," she added at Maddy's questioning look. "It's pretty hard to keep secrets in a town the size of Sweetheart.''

Accepting the offering, Maddy smiled, thinking that what the pretty blond woman said wasn't quite true. John Taggart had kept his love for this woman a secret for a very long time. ''Allison Montgomery, I presume?''

''You're good. Guess Pete has told you all about me, huh?''

''Yes, he mentioned you at dinner the other night, as a matter of fact.''

Allison rimmed the edge of her punch glass with her fingertip. ''Pete doesn't like me. Never has. He thinks I'm too pushy and career oriented. He doesn't like that in a woman.''

Maddy found the woman's comment disturbing, though it was no more than she'd already suspected. ''What is it you do for a living that Pete finds so objectionable?''

''I own a catering business, but it's not the business that he finds objectionable, just the fact that I'm a woman who'd rather have a career than a marriage. I'd dearly love to have a child, just not the husband to go along with it.''

Allison's story was a familiar one. Many of the working women she knew, both single and divorced, didn't want the trappings of marriage. But many desired a child. Of course, unlike her, most weren't foolish enough to go out and get themselves pregnant.

''Your biological clock is ticking, I take it.''

She shrugged. "I guess. I was an only child and the idea of having children, of being part of a large family, appeals to me."

"But not a husband?"

Her gaze drifted across the room to where Pete was standing engrossed in conversation with Sweetheart's mayor and town barber, Bobby Orrback. "Well, not one like Pete anyway. The man's too controlling by far. You'll find that out if you stick around long enough. He objected to his late wife working and—" Allison shook her head. "I'm sorry. I know it's not polite of me to be telling you all of this. John tells me I have a bad habit of running off at the mouth."

Maddy arched a brow. "And you don't mind him saying that?"

The woman laughed. "Heavens, no! John and I have known each other forever. We're practically like brother and sister. And you know how siblings often speak their minds? Plus, he's my best friend, so I guess that gives him the right to point out a few of my flaws. Just as long as he doesn't get carried away."

"Don't believe half of what this woman says," John told Maddy as he stepped up to join their conversation, his eyes filled with warmth as they fell on the woman next to her, who was grinning broadly. He looked just like a lovesick puppy. Why couldn't Allison Montgomery see what was right before her eyes?

"Allison is a horrible gossip, and she never has anything nice to say about anyone, especially me."

Maddy grinned when the woman punched her best friend in the arm, and said, "I told you, John, that as soon as I think of something nice to say, you'll be the first to know."

With a wink at Maddy, she added, "I'm going over to talk Mark into giving me his recipe for bourbon balls. Nice meeting you, Maddy."

John's heart was on his sleeve as he watched Allison walk away, and Maddy felt sorry for him. Unrequited love was a terrible waste, and she had a feeling that she'd soon be learning that lesson firsthand.

"Allison's lovely. She seems to be quite businessminded."

"There's a lot more to life than business, Maddy. Too bad Ally hasn't learned that yet." Pete strolled up just then, and Maddy was spared from commenting. Not that she had much to offer on the subject, for she and Allison were somewhat alike in their career aspirations.

Why were the Taggart men so backward in their thinking when it came to women in the workplace? she wondered.

The two men exchanged a few words about the weather and party guests, then John disappeared in the general direction of the pretty blonde, leaving Maddy and Pete alone in a room full of people.

"Sorry to be gone so long," he said. "I needed to speak to a few people I've been neglecting for far too long." How had he allowed himself to become so self-absorbed, so self-pitying? Some of the people here tonight—Bobby Orrback, for one—had been friends of his since grade school, and he hadn't spoken more than a few obligatory words to them in years. Pete was ashamed of his past behavior and vowed to rectify things.

"That's all right. I had a perfectly lovely talk with Allison Montgomery."

Pete shook his head in disgust. "Allison's tearing my brother up inside, and she doesn't even know it."

"She thinks you don't like her. Is that true?"

"Ally's all right for the most part," he conceded. "But she's pushy and opinionated, and she's been leading my brother on a merry chase for years. I guess I'd like her a whole lot better if she'd put John out of his misery and declare her undying love for the poor guy."

Maddy smiled softly. "Why, Pete Taggart, I think you're a romantic at heart. Who would have ever guessed?"

He tweaked the end of her nose and smiled. "And I think you've been drinking too much of this eggnog." He removed the glass from her hands. "You shouldn't be drinking this anyway. It's got rum in it."

"But I like it," she protested. "I was about to fetch another cup."

"It's not good for the baby," he whispered.

"Allison was right. You're far too controlling. And I'll thank you very much not to act like my parent, Pete Taggart. I'm a little old to be lectured to, and I'm perfectly capable of deciding what and how much to drink.''

"Suit yourself. But recent studies have shown that alcohol's not good for a fetus.''

Aware of that particular study, Maddy knew it was true and couldn't fault him for calling her on it. Handing him the cup, she said, "I concede that you might be correct, but you still mustn't hover over me like a mother hen.'' Though admittedly she found his concern endearing.

He flashed a grin. "Come on. There's someone I'd like you to meet.''

"The surgeon general?'' she quipped.

"Nope. Ella Grady. Ella spotted you earlier from across the room, and she's dying to meet someone from New York City.''

A moment later, Maddy found herself face-to-face with the shortest woman she had ever met. Ella Grady was as fat as she was short, had permanent dimples etched into her round face from smiling so much, and curly hair the color of cotton. If ever there was a candidate for Mrs. Claus, Ella was it.

"You know, dear,'' Ella said, "I was just telling Pete that I'd love to go to New York City and see Rockefeller Center and that huge Christmas tree I see on TV every year. It all looks so very lovely and festive. But I doubt at my age, and with my arthritis, I'll ever get there. Of course, there's something to be said for small-town living, don't you agree?''

Sensing a trap, Maddy chose her words carefully.

"From the small portion I've seen of it, Sweetheart is a lovely town."

"Maddy's not big on country living, Ella. She's a city girl," Pete explained, wondering why the words burned his throat like bad whiskey.

The older woman wasn't fazed by the remark. "People don't set down roots because of cities. They stay because of who's living there. Isn't that right, Maddy?"

Maddy hesitated a moment, gazing at Pete out of the corner of her eye, before saying, "I suppose that's true."

"Of course it's true. I bet if you got to know the folks in this town better, saw what a wonderful place Sweetheart is to live, you'd never want to go back to New York City. Seems like an awfully cold place to me, and I'm not talking about the weather."

"Did I happen to mention that Ella's also our resident matchmaker here in Sweetheart? She won't be happy until all the Taggart men are hog-tied and wed." Pete winked at Ella, and Maddy felt her face warm.

"*Humph!* You Taggarts are a contrary bunch. I've about given up on the lot of you." Ella turned her attention back to the young woman. "We need new blood in this community, girl. I hope you'll think about staying on."

"I appreciate the invitation, Miss Grady, but I'm on my way to visit my sister in Leadville and can't stay much longer."

"*Pshaw!* Leadville's not that far. If you lived here,

you could visit your sister any ol' time you wanted. And it's Ella, not Miss Grady. Lord, girl, but you'll make me feel as old as Methuselah, if you insist on calling me Miss Grady."

Maddy couldn't help but like the outspoken woman. She was kind and well-meaning, despite the fact that she said whatever was on her mind. "Thank you, Ella. I appreciate your hospitality, but I'll be leaving here as soon as my car is repaired and the roads are safe to drive." Willis had finally towed her car into town.

"Well, if this young man allows you to do that, he's a lot dumber than I think." She turned on her heel and waddled over to the other side of the room, leaving Maddy to stare openmouthed after her.

Pete stared thoughtfully at Maddy before taking her hand and leading her out of the crowded room and up the stairs. It was time they had a serious discussion.

"Where are we going?" she asked. "Aren't the guest rooms up here?" Her heart started pounding at the possibilities, and it was anticipation, not dread, she was feeling.

Pete had been making teasing comments and sexual innuendos for days. What if he decided to act on them?

What if she did?

He nodded. "Yes, but most of the guests are at the party so I think we're safe."

Safe with Pete Taggart? Maddy didn't think so.

When they reached a small, quiet sitting room decorated with heavy, dark Victorian-style furniture, Pete lit the logs in the fireplace, adding instant warmth and atmosphere to the attractive floral-papered room.

"I've been living alone too long, I guess. I like the quiet. That constant humming of voices downstairs was beginning to get on my nerves. It's much nicer up here, don't you think?"

"Aren't you glad you came to the party? You seemed to be having a good time."

He joined her on the rose-velvet settee. "I'm glad I came with you," he admitted, and her face lit with a smile that shot straight to his heart. He paused a moment to gather his thoughts, then said, "Uh, there's something I've been thinking about, Maddy, something I've been wanting to talk to you about."

Maddy's brows drew together. "What is it? You look upset. Did something happen?"

Something happened, all right. Maddy happened. And Pete wasn't upset, he was nervous. He'd come to a decision tonight—a decision that had surprised him almost as much as it was likely to surprise Maddy. Ella's words had given him the impetus to act on an idea he'd been mulling over for days, and long, lonely nights.

"I realized tonight that the perfect solution to your problem has been right before us all along, and I was just too blind to see it before now."

A shiver of apprehension shimmied down Maddy's spine. Pete looked serious and intent about whatever he had on his mind, and she was afraid to ask what that was, but she had to know. "A solution to my problem?" He could only mean the baby.

He took her hand, which was growing clammier by the second, and began caressing her fingers. "We get along pretty good, Maddy. And I think you'll agree that there's chemistry between us."

She gulped at the understatement, at the fear of what was to come.

"So..." He cleared his throat, making Maddy even more nervous. "I was thinking that it might not be such a bad idea if you were to marry me. I'm not joking this time, Maddy. I want you to be my wife."

Chapter Six

Maddy sat stunned, her heart hammering, the roar in her ears deafening, unable to believe that Pete Taggart had just proposed marriage.

Perhaps he had dipped into the eggnog too many times himself, she thought. But the odd thing was he seemed perfectly serious and sober.

"Why do you want to marry me?" she asked. "We hardly know each other, and I'm carrying another man's child."

"The baby's father is out of the picture, right?" When she nodded, he said, "I'd raise the baby as my own, Maddy. There'd never be any doubt as to who his or her father is. The child would be loved.

"And you're right—we haven't known each other long. But we seem compatible. And marrying me would solve your immediate problem, you've got to admit that."

She sighed deeply. *And it would create a host of others.*

"But you don't love me. We don't love each

other," she quickly amended, afraid her feelings for him were as transparent as the lovely etched glass in the windows, afraid he would see the love she felt shining in her eyes.

Pete had said the child would be loved; he hadn't mentioned a thing about the child's mother.

"I won't lie to you, Maddy. I don't think I'm capable of ever loving another woman. Bethany's death decimated me, left a void deep inside me, an anger that only now is starting to dissipate. But I care for you. I'll take care of you and the baby. I swear it."

Her heart took a nosedive while her hand went to her abdomen, and she gently caressed the tiny life growing inside her. "It's because of the baby, isn't it? Because you want a child?"

"I won't deny it. I was devastated when I lost my wife and child. I've always wanted to be a father. I think I'd make a good one, and I'd like the chance to prove it."

From what she knew of Pete Taggart, she couldn't argue that point. He was a caring individual who took his responsibilities to heart.

But did she merely want to be just someone's responsibility? Shouldn't she expect the father of her child to love her? And could she settle for anything less, knowing how she felt about him?

And there was also the matter of her career. Pete Taggart had made it clear how he felt about career-oriented women. It would be a stumbling block between them, for she had no intention of allowing any man to run her life. "I have a career in advertising.

You've made your feelings on women in the workplace pretty clear. And they weren't all that flattering, as I recall. Have you changed your mind then?''

He shook his head. "I don't think wives and mothers should work outside the home. A man should be the sole support of his family. But I also know that your career is important to you.

"And since we're coming at this marriage in a very untraditional manner, I've decided that it would be all right if you continued to work part-time, here in Sweetheart. You'd have to give up that high-powered job in New York City and agree to live here, full-time. I'd expect that much of a commitment from you.''

She opened her mouth to protest, to tell him he was arrogant and nuts, a true Neanderthal in every sense of the word, then shut it again. There was no use arguing with Pete until she had thought things through, given his proposal due consideration. She felt she owed him that much, for saving her and her baby's life. And for offering an honorable solution to her predicament.

And it was likely her position at Lassiter, Owens and Cumberland would soon be terminated. The partners would find a convenient excuse to let her go. And if they couldn't, they'd invent one. That's how things were done in corporate America. Neat and tidy. No messes. She'd be given a golden parachute—a huge severance package that would appease David's guilt—along with a letter of recommendation. It would all be very civilized.

Staring into Pete's dark blue eyes and earnest face, she realized he was far more civilized than those three bastards back in New York that she'd dedicated herself to for the past six years.

Reaching up, she placed her palm on his cheek. "You've given me a great deal to think about. I'll need time to consider your proposal."

Hope filled his eyes, and he clasped her hand and kissed it. "Don't take too long, Maddy. The baby's not showing yet, and it would be easy enough at this point to let folks think it's mine...ours. Of course, my family would have to be told the truth, but other than that..." He shrugged. "I've led a pretty reclusive life, so most of the townsfolk would accept whatever we tell them."

No shame. No embarrassment. No emotional attachment. On his part, anyway. It would all be so...*polite,* Maddy thought. "I need to think this over carefully. There's a lot more at stake here than just my career or your desire for a child. I've got to do what's best for my baby. That has to be the most important consideration."

Even more than her love for him.

MADDY AWOKE CHRISTMAS morning and was no closer to making a decision regarding Pete's proposal than she'd been the week before, though he'd been gently prodding her. He'd used every persuasive tactic he knew, including dragging out his cradle from the attic—the one his great-grandfather had fashioned with his own hands—and restoring it before the fire every night.

She had watched his strong hands glide lovingly over the dark wood as he sanded and polished it, and she wondered what they would feel like moving over her naked flesh in a similar fashion. The persistent, too-vivid thoughts created a yearning deep within her that wouldn't abate. She ached for Pete Taggart in the most elemental and shameful way.

"Damn you, Pete!" she whispered, then drew the quilt up over her head. The very quilt that had foretold of a marriage between them.

"Damn you, Maggie Taggart! This is all your fault. You and that stupid quilt legend have made my life miserable." Punching her pillow, she reconsidered. "No. It's really Pete's fault for making me fall in love with him, for making me care."

But Maddy knew whose fault it really was that her life had become so confused and chaotic. It was hers. She'd been the one to get pregnant. She'd been the one to insist on driving through a snowstorm. She'd been the one to find Pete's grandmother's quilt. And she'd been the one to fall in love with a man who would never love her in return, who only wanted to marry her because of the baby she was carrying, who was so pathetically honest in his feelings that she cried every time she thought about it.

Rufus, who was lying in front of the fire, whimpered in his sleep, then quieted. Maddy envied him for being a dog, who had only to worry about where his next meal was coming from. "Life sucks, Rufus, old boy," she whispered.

Sitting cross-legged in the middle of the bed, Maddy clutched the pillow to her chest and stared out the window at the falling snow. It had been snowing for days. The brief respite they'd had the day of Mark's party was just a memory. The only saving grace was that the electricity and phones had been restored, making their day to day routine a little easier.

Of course, that meant she had no excuse for not phoning her sister. Mary Beth had probably been trying to reach her at the apartment and would be frantic with worry by now. She had to contact her, no matter how difficult the conversation, or her admission, was going to be.

The phone beside the bed called to Maddy, and she reached for it, dialing her sister's number before she could chicken out and change her mind.

Suddenly Mary Beth's voice came through the receiver, bringing tears to her eyes. "Merry Christmas, Mary Beth. It's Maddy."

The relief in her sister's voice was evident, making her feel even guiltier. "Maddy! Thank God! I've been trying to reach you for days. Where are you? I've been worried sick."

"As a matter of fact, I'm in Colorado."

"You're kidding? Were you coming to surprise me for Christmas? Are you at the airport? Shall Lyle come fetch you?"

It was just like Mary Beth to think the best of her.

Maddy shook her head, then realized her sister couldn't see her. "I'm staying with a friend. I got caught in a blizzard and wrecked my car. We had more snow last night and the roads are still a mess."

"And where is here?" her sister demanded, still miffed by the sound of it. Not that Maddy could blame her. If the shoe had been on the other foot, she'd have been just as concerned.

"Sweetheart," she replied. "But we're actually several miles outside of town on a cattle ranch."

"How long have you been there?"

Maddy took a deep breath. "Almost two weeks."

"Two weeks! You've been in Colorado two weeks and you haven't called me?"

"The phones were just restored a couple of days ago. And…and, well, there was another reason I couldn't call."

"Are you being held against your will?"

Maddy smiled at her sister's alarm. It was so like Mary Beth to conjure up a frightening scenario. Lyle blamed her behavior on all the evening news magazine shows she watched. "No, Mary Beth, I'm not a hostage. I haven't been kidnapped or held against my will. Actually, I've been treated very well, considering everything.

"I—" She swallowed. "I've got something to tell you, and I know you're going to be disappointed in me."

There was a frustrated sigh, a significant pause on the other end of the phone, then Maddy's sister said in a gentle voice that Maddy had come to love and rely on so much, "I love you, Mad. You know that. If you're in trouble, I want to help. You are in trouble, aren't you?"

"I'm pregnant, Mary Beth."

"So am I."

"What?" Maddy squealed into the phone, unable to contain her excitement, and her sister laughed. "Oh, Mary Beth. I'm so happy for you and Lyle. When did you find out?"

"Just a few days ago. That's why I've been calling and trying to reach you. I'm finally going to have a baby, Mad. And now you are, too. Isn't it wonderful? We can make so many plans together."

"Yes, it's wonderful." At least it was in Mary Beth's case. "But our situations are a bit different, in case you've forgotten. You're married and I'm not."

"Hmm. Are you with the father of your child now? Has he refused to marry you?"

"Pete Taggart isn't the father of my child. David Lassiter is. And he wants nothing to do with the baby. He told me to have an abortion."

Her sister's shocked gasp came as no surprise. The woman was religious, though she didn't try to foist her beliefs onto others. Maddy had always been grateful for that. "Lassiter, as in your boss?" she asked.

"Yes. And it's likely I've already been given the boot. But please don't ask me for details right now.

"Actually, the reason I'm calling is that the man

whose home I've been living in, Pete Taggart, has asked me to marry him.''

A pause ensued. ''Run that by me again. The father of your child doesn't want the baby, but the man you've been stranded with during a blizzard does?''

''It's a long and very complicated story.'' One she didn't fully understand herself.

''I bet. Do you love him? Because he sounds like a regular Sir Galahad. A real knight in shining armor.''

Maddy sighed. ''Yes. I'm afraid I do.''

''That's wonderful! So what's the problem? Marry him. Be happy.''

''There's a hitch. He doesn't love me. He only wants the child.''

''But you just said he wanted to marry you. Sounds to me as if he wants you.''

If only that were true.

''What should I do, Mary Beth? I'm so confused. I've been trying to come up with an answer for days now, and I'm not any closer to making a decision.''

''First things first. Take a deep breath and think about this whole situation logically. You love Pete Taggart, you need a father for your baby, and I'm not convinced that he's indifferent to you. No man would saddle himself with a wife and child unless he had feelings, strong feelings.''

''If he has any feelings for me, it's because of the quilt.'' She quickly explained about the legend of the wedding ring quilt, and her sister burst out laughing.

''You think a man would marry you because of a

stupid quilt legend? Get real, Maddy. I thought you had more sense than that. Your hormones must be totally out of whack.''

They were. Maddy had been crying at the drop of a hat over the stupidest things, but her hormones had nothing to do with how she felt about the legend. ''I'm telling you there's truth to the legend, Mary Beth. It foretold of a marriage, then Pete proposes out of the blue. There can be no other explanation. I don't believe in coincidences of any kind.''

''Listen, Maddy. I have to go now. Lyle says Merry Christmas, but I have to get off the phone to go to church. Give me your phone number and we'll talk again very soon.'' Maddy heaved a sigh and did as her sister requested, congratulating her again on the news of her pregnancy. She promised to call when she'd made her decision regarding Pete.

Maddy felt like telling Mary Beth not to hold her breath.

''MERRY CHRISTMAS!'' Pete said when Maddy entered the kitchen a short time later. ''I'd almost given up on you showing up for breakfast. Hope you're hungry. I've got bacon, pancakes and scrambled eggs warming in the oven. And there's hot syrup in the pitcher.''

Maddy's eyes widened as her gaze landed on the kitchen table, which had been set for two. ''You made breakfast for me?''

''I figured you were tired, so I went ahead and did

the honors.'' He pulled out a chair for her, and her sister's comment about Sir Galahad came to mind. ''Come sit down. I hope you're hungry.''

She smiled softly. No man had ever cooked breakfast for her before. Or asked her to marry him, for that matter. She was deeply touched and felt like crying again, but willed herself not to. The last time Pete had caught her crying over a glass of spilled milk, he'd looked at her with such anguish that she didn't have the heart to put him through such an ordeal again. She was finding out that the big, tough-as-nails rancher was in reality a softy.

''I'm famished,'' she said. ''And it smells absolutely wonderful. I thought you said you couldn't cook.''

''Said I didn't like to cook. There's a difference. And I figured I needed to impress you with the fact that I'm a—what is it they call men who do everything?—a Renaissance man?''

She laughed aloud, loving him more in that moment than she ever thought possible to love anyone. ''Thank you. I'm definitely impressed. Mmm,'' she added, after tasting the pancakes. ''These are yummy. I'll be as fat as a cow if you keep this up.''

''Don't be duped by all those TV commercials and ads you read in magazines. Men like women with curves and a little meat on their bones. Some of those supermodels look like they haven't eaten for years. They all look anorexic.''

"Goodness! You really are trying to butter me up."

"This is nothing," he said, grinning like a small boy with a terribly big secret. "Just wait till we open presents."

Her eyes widened in dismay. "Presents! But I haven't anything for you, Pete. How could you go shopping when the roads are still in such poor shape?"

"Like any good Eagle Scout, I improvised. Now hurry up and eat, so we can get on to the good stuff."

Twenty minutes later they were seated on the floor beneath the gaily decorated Christmas tree. Maddy couldn't take her eyes off the antique cradle that Pete had restored so handsomely. It was as singular as he was.

If she closed her eyes, she could almost believe they were a real couple, married and in love with each other, sharing their first Christmas morning together. It was a lovely dream—one, Maddy realized, she wanted.

But how could she make it come true? How could she make Pete fall in love with her?

She'd never been one for artifice or feminine wiles, but maybe it was time to start. After all, she'd landed million-dollar accounts for the advertising firm with little or no problem, selling herself as much as the idea.

How hard could it be to land one indifferent and difficult man?

She did so love a challenge!

"What are you smiling about, Miz Potter, ma'am? You've got the look of the devil in your eyes. Should I be scared?"

Maddy blushed, glad Pete didn't know what she'd been thinking. "I was just thinking how lovely the tree is, the whole scenario of Christmas morning, with the snow falling outside the window and a crackling fire in the hearth. I feel like I'm in one of those old movies. Remember *Christmas in Connecticut?*"

"Nope," Pete said, shaking his head and dropping down beside her on the rug. "I'm not much for old movies.

"Maddy—" his tone suddenly became serious "—I haven't wanted to put too much pressure on you, but I'm hoping that you've given my marriage proposal some thought." His look was hopeful and expectant.

"I've thought of little else, Pete Taggart, you can be sure of that. And I've got the dark circles under my eyes to prove it."

He grinned, drawing a present from behind his back. "Maybe this will sway you to my way of thinking then." He handed her the small velvet box, which she opened with trembling fingers. "It was my mother's, and her mother's before that. I hope you like it."

The diamond-and-ruby ring sparkled as brilliantly as the twinkling lights on the tree, totally captivating

Maddy as she thought of the generations of Taggart women who had worn it. Her eyes filled with tears for what it symbolized: love, commitment, sharing a life together.

"It's exquisite. I—I don't know what to say. I have no gift for you."

"Say you'll be my wife." He placed his palm on her stomach. "And the only gift I want is resting inside you at this very moment. This will be our child, Maddy. Yours and mine." He drew her into his arms and kissed her, and she melted into him like warm butter on toast.

Easing her down on the braided rug, he brushed the loose strands of hair away from her face with gentle fingers. "I want you, Maddy. I want you in my bed, in my life. Please say you'll marry me."

She gazed into his eyes and saw tenderness and affection. He cared for her, she knew. It wasn't love, but maybe in time that would come. In the meantime, the love she felt for him would have to be enough.

Taking a deep breath, she said, "Yes, I'll marry you. Now kiss me again before I change my mind."

"You won't be sorry," he said, placing the ring on her finger, and she prayed he was right.

Plunging his tongue deep inside her mouth, Pete made Maddy forget everything but the warm hands on her breasts and the clever fingers making short work of the buttons on her jeans.

He pushed up her sweater, freeing her swollen breasts from the confines of her black lace bra, lapping at her hardened nipples, before drawing them into his mouth and sucking. Every nerve ending in Maddy's body short-circuited.

"You taste good," he whispered, trailing kisses down the underside of her breasts, her stomach, down her abdomen, where he tenderly caressed her slightly swollen tummy, dipping his tongue into her belly button and making her cry out.

"Pete, you're torturing me!" she declared between gasps of breath.

"As you've tortured me these many nights, sweetheart," he said, pulling down her jeans and underpants and baring her body to his view. "I want to taste all of you, Maddy. Open to me. Let me love you."

Yes! Please love me! Love me as I love you.

Nudging her legs apart gently, he tasted the very essence of her, delving deep, while lifting her off the ground to appease his hunger.

With every stroke of Pete's tongue, Maddy soared higher and higher, clasping his head and urging him on, acting every bit the wanton woman she suddenly felt. "Oh, oh!" she whimpered, then released the moan from deep within her throat as he brought her to a stunning, earth-shattering climax that had her soaring to the heavens.

Afterward Pete drew her into his arms and cradled her to his chest, kissing her hair, her neck, her cheeks. "I wanted to make it good for you, Maddy. Was it? Did I please you?"

She nodded, too stunned to say anything. Finally, when her breathing returned to normal and she could speak again, she whispered, "I've never experienced anything like it. I've never done that."

He grinned. "Damn, but that makes me feel good."

"But…but…what about you? Don't you want to finish what we started?" She was almost disappointed he didn't take her all the way. She wanted to be with him, become part of him. She wanted to feel him deep inside her, feel his seed spill into her. Because this time, she knew it would be right.

"I want to wait to consummate our relationship until we're married, Maddy. I want to do this whole marriage thing right. I'll call Reverend Andrews tomorrow and get the ball rolling for our wedding ceremony. Then we'll have us a proper wedding night. It'll be worth the wait, you'll see."

Of that she had no doubt. Caressing his cheek, she said, "You're really a very old-fashioned kind of man. I think that's very sweet and terribly refreshing in this day and age." He had put her needs before his, had considered her feelings above his own. He had been totally unselfish and caring.

Is it any wonder that I love you, Pete Taggart?

"Our father taught us boys to cherish women, but also to be respectful of them. I figured you'd want to wait till we tied the knot before we went any further." He placed her hand on his hardened member.

"But there's no doubt that I want you, sweetheart. Want you real bad."

"But, Pete, if you want me now, I wouldn't say no." Her smile was teasing, his tortured.

With a groan, he pulled down her sweater and yanked up her pants. "Don't tempt me, woman. I'm only a man."

She grinned. "Yes, I know. That's what I'm counting on."

Chapter Seven

Entering the back door of The Sweetheart Inn, Pete found Mark elbow deep in concentration and wedding preparations, putting the finishing touches on a three-layer white-frosted cake complete with bride, groom and pink rosettes. It was perfect, and Maddy was going to love it.

They were to be married that night—New Year's Eve—at the inn, with family and a few close friends in attendance. Maddy had asked the only woman under sixty she knew in town—Allison Montgomery—to be her maid of honor, much to Pete's dismay. Maddy's sister, Mary Beth, had not been able to attend on such short notice, due to her husband's job as Leadville's chief of police. John would act as best man, Sarah as flower girl, while Evan would bear the ring. The kids were almost as excited as he was.

Pete had done a lot of soul-searching in the past few days, weighed all the pros and cons, and he knew without a doubt that marrying Maddy was the right thing for both of them. He cared about her a great deal, wanted what was best for her, and needed to protect her. Why that was, he hadn't asked himself, fearful of what the answer might be.

"Looks like you've got everything under control, little brother," Pete told Mark, who looked up and scowled fiercely at him.

"You know I hate an audience when I'm working, so get lost for a while, okay? I'm busy, and I've still got a lot to do before the reception tonight." A mountain of cream puffs stood on the stainless steel countertop waiting to be filled with the chef's famous salmon mousse. Finger sandwiches and hors d'oeuvres had already been prepared and were now stored in the large Sub-Zero refrigerator, awaiting to-night's event.

Pete ignored his brother's request for solitude and pulled out a chair, straddling it. "Maddy's doing some last-minute shopping with Allison—women things, I suspect—so I'm kinda at loose ends for the time being. Thought I'd keep you company." He was nervous, but he wasn't about to admit that to anyone, especially his little brother.

Mark and John thought he had nerves of steel, because most things usually just rolled off his back, like water off a duck. Little did they know that the prospect of getting married again terrified Pete. Not the institution itself, but because his feelings for Maddy were much stronger than he'd realized. He was in danger of losing his heart, of opening himself up to hurt, and he couldn't allow that to happen. Not again.

"Where's John? He's your best man. Why don't you go keep him company?"

As if conjured up by the innkeeper's words, the door suddenly opened, admitting a blast of cold air and the other Taggart brother. "Well, looks like all the usual suspects are here," John quipped, throwing off his sheepskin-lined leather jacket and pulling up a chair. His cheeks were ruddy from the cold. "Got any coffee? I'm freezing my *cajones* off. Had to go and pick up my suit at the dry cleaners for tonight's shindig."

Pete filled two ceramic mugs with the steaming liquid and handed his brother one. The aroma of French roast filled the large room. "I realize this wedding is short notice for everyone, and...well, I appreciate you both putting things aside to help me out."

Mark was allowing them to stay in the bridal suite at no charge. He had closed the inn for the evening, at great expense to himself. It was New Year's Eve and he could have made a small fortune had he remained open. Pete felt somewhat guilty, but extremely grateful, for his sacrifice. He wanted everything to be perfect. Maddy deserved no less.

"I hope you know what you're doing, Pete," John said, sipping his coffee and becoming as somber and serious as a minister about to deliver Sunday's sermon. "You haven't known Maddy Potter very long, and marrying someone who's carrying another man's child is only asking for trouble. What if the guy shows up and decides he wants his kid back? What then?''

"The guy's a bastard," Pete told him, unable to keep the venomous anger out of his voice. "He's some rich executive idiot who wants nothing to do with the child." And if David Lassiter did show his face in Sweetheart, Pete thought, he intended to rearrange it for him.

How could any man throw away his own child? How could any man in his right mind give up a woman like Maddy?

Mark paused in what he was doing and looked up, his eyes filled with concern. "John's right, you know. Are you sure you've given this enough thought? Don't get me wrong. I like Maddy. I think she's a terrific woman. But like John said, you haven't known each other long. And trust me, custody battles are no picnic. I speak from experience."

Pete wished now that he'd never taken his brothers into his confidence about Maddy's pregnancy. They were overprotective, alarmists by nature, always thinking of the worst possible scenarios.

Why couldn't they just be happy for him and wish him well?

"So what if we haven't known each other long?" he tossed back. "You and Pam knew each other eight years before you were married, and you still got divorced. What's that old saying? Familiarity breeds contempt?"

Mark shrugged, looking ill at ease at the reminder.

"I'm just worried about you. John and I don't want to see you get hurt."

"And you've already admitted that you don't love the woman," the vet reminded his brother. "What kind of groundwork are you laying for a successful marriage? The baby's not going to be enough to bind the two of you together. It won't make up for a loveless marriage. I think you're going to regret this hasty decision, Pete."

The rancher's eyes hardened into sapphires, and his lips slashed into a thin line. "Fortunately I don't give a tinker's damn what you think, what either one of you bozos think. I'm marrying the woman, and that's that." Rising to his feet, Pete walked to the door, then paused and looked back.

"And I'd appreciate it if you two would keep your opinions to yourselves. I'm old enough to make my own decisions about what I want to do with my life, and with whom I want to do it. I don't want Maddy hearing your comments and being hurt by them."

The door slammed shut, and John let loose a shrill whistle, then he grinned from ear to ear. "Methinks our big brother isn't being totally honest with himself."

Mark licked confectioner's frosting off his fingers and looked askance. "What d'ya mean? He seems to know his own mind. He sure as hell was adamant about marrying the woman. We've said our piece. Now I think we should just butt out."

"Pete might know his own mind, but I'll bet you

ten bucks he doesn't know his own heart. The fool's in love. I'd bet money on it.''

Mark considered his brother's comments, then burst out laughing. ''Things could get pretty interesting around here in the next few months, couldn't they?''

''What was it Pop always said? 'It takes a woman to make life interesting.' You know, I do believe the old man was right.''

ALLISON HELD UP a sheer black nightie for Maddy's inspection and grinned at the woman's horrified expression. ''This is just the ticket for a passion-filled wedding night. It leaves absolutely nothing to the imagination, which is good, because I don't think your fiancé has much of one. Pete sees everything in black and white, which makes this gown the perfect choice.''

Maddy was no prude, but she felt her cheeks warm just the same and had the sudden urge to burst forth with a chorus of *Auld Lang Syne.*

Several of the customers at Bootsie's Boutique were staring in their direction, trying to listen in on their conversation. ''I'm trying to keep this wedding low profile, Allison,'' she whispered, taking the garment from the amused blonde's hands and stuffing it under her arm and out of sight. ''But I'll keep your suggestion in mind.''

If she didn't like Allison Montgomery so much, and wasn't so indebted to her for agreeing to be part of the wedding on such short notice, Maddy might have been tempted to walk out the door. She definitely didn't need any more stress at the moment.

But she definitely needed the nightgown. It was just what she deemed essential to knock the rancher's socks off. Not that he'd be wearing any tonight. If she had her way, Pete Taggart would be wearing only his sexiest smile. The thought sent a shiver down her spine.

"Your expression is downright lascivious, girl. You could be arrested in a town like this for wearing a smile like that. Sheriff Dobbs is very strict about such things."

Maddy's face crimsoned again. "Hush! You're terrible. Now let's finish up and go get something to eat. I'm starving."

"Now that you're eating for two?"

Maddy looked around quickly, but fortunately no one had heard the woman's comment. Did everyone in Sweetheart speak so bluntly? First Ella, now Allison. "Who told you?" It had to be one of Pete's brothers. They were the only ones who knew. "It was John, wasn't it?"

"I hope you don't mind," the young woman said, looking somewhat contrite as she led Maddy to the front of the store to pay for her purchases. "John and I are very close, and we share most everything. It would have been hard for him to keep this a secret from me. But I promise not to breathe a word to anyone. I think it's all very exciting."

After paying for the nightgown and other assorted undergarments, Maddy and Allison made their way down the main street of town toward the Java Connection. The coffeehouse served sandwiches and salads as well as coffee, and Maddy needed sustenance. And fast.

"Are you sure you're not rushing into things?" Allison asked, once they were seated with their coffee, blowing into her cup before taking a sip. "I know it's none of my business, but I like you, Maddy, and I don't want to see you making a big mistake."

"A bigger mistake, don't you mean? I've already made quite a whopper." She toyed with the red-skinned potato salad on her plate, pushing it from one side to the other.

"I think you're lucky." Allison's expression grew wistful. "I'd love to be in your shoes. Pregnant and about to have my first child. If you'd just leave Pete out of the equation, everything would be perfect."

"I appreciate your concern, but I know what I'm doing, so you needn't worry about me. Pete Taggart's a good man. He's been very kind to me. I think we'll do well together."

Allison hesitated a moment, then said, "If you want to tell me to shut up, go right ahead, but—do you love him?"

The bride-to-be heaved a deep, heartfelt sigh. "Yes. I do. More than I ever thought possible to love anyone."

"Gee, that's too bad."

Maddy nodded in resignation. "Yes, I know."

"What about your career? Are you just going to

chuck it out the window? Because I'm telling you right now that Pete'll never stand for your working. His late wife, Bethany, confided that he was adamantly opposed to her working at the radio station. It had put a serious strain on their relationship, especially after she found out she was pregnant.''

"We've already come to a compromise about my working. I intend to set up an advertising and promotions business here in Sweetheart. In fact,'' she said, and smiled excitedly, "I've already got my first two accounts—The Sweetheart Inn and Taggart's Veterinary Clinic.'' She was overjoyed and extremely grateful when the two men suggested that she help them with their businesses. Pete wasn't aware of his brothers' generosity as yet.

The blonde's blue eyes grew troubled. "The Taggart brothers are all great guys. I love them dearly. But they were raised by a patriarch who thought women belonged up on a pedestal. Donna Reed was Jack Taggart's ideal of womanhood. He was into that little woman thing in a big way.'' Allison repressed a shudder.

Maddy couldn't help laughing, though some of what her friend said troubled her. "I'm a modern woman, and Pete knows it. I intend for this marriage to be a partnership, not a dictatorship.'' Her father had been controlling and dictatorial, and Maddy had no intention of living her life under those conditions.

Allison covered her hand and squeezed. "Good luck, Maddy. I think you're going to need it.''

IT HAD BEEN THE SHORTEST wedding ceremony in Sweetheart's history, or so the Reverend James Andrews from Trinity Methodist Church had claimed during the signing of the wedding certificate.

Pete intended to make up for that by having the longest, hottest wedding night in the history of Colorado. Just as soon as he could get through the reception.

"Did I tell you how beautiful you look tonight, Mrs. Taggart?" he whispered to his new bride standing next to him. They had just performed the obligatory dance and were now taking a breather.

She blushed prettily. "I bet you say that to all the pregnant brides."

"Can we dispense with the cutting of the cake and go directly to the wedding night?"

Maddy laughed, feeling her cheeks warm and her blood heat. "Wearing such a beautiful gown would make any woman look good. Thank you for allowing me to borrow your mother's wedding dress, Pete. It was so thoughtful of you to think of it." The antique satin and lace gown was exquisite and made her feel like a fairy-tale princess. Fortunately, she'd already found her Prince Charming.

"Mom wouldn't have wanted it any other way, especially since she never had any daughters to pass it on to. She would have wanted you to have it."

"The gown is a bit tight in the bust. I hope no one noticed." Actually, it was very tight in the bust, and a lot of people had noticed, mostly men. Maddy had done a great deal of blushing and folding her arms over her chest all evening. For a woman who'd never thought of her bosom as large, she now felt like Dolly Parton.

Pete noticed, too, and he couldn't wait to unwrap those luscious, pink-tipped mounds and have his way. "I'd tell you what I was thinking about your breasts, but then I'd have to hide behind your skirts all evening or embarrass myself in front of a room full of people."

Laughter bubbled up her throat. Maddy had never felt so happy. And even if it was all an illusion, it was her dream come true. "You're incorrigible, Mr. Taggart. I think I'm ready to cut the cake and head upstairs to make use of that large whirlpool tub in our suite. I might even let you wash my back, if you're a good boy." She ran her finger down his leg suggestively, pleased when she felt him shiver.

Her words and action had the desired effect—Pete stiffened like a tree trunk. "Damn, Maddy. You did that on purpose. Now what am I supposed to do?"

Eyes twinkling, she retorted, "Well, if you don't know by now, I'm not going to tell you."

Ella approached just then, and Pete took off like a Teflon-coated bullet for the kitchen. "Mercy, where is that boy heading in such a hurry? He must be famished again. I swear, those Taggart boys have such big appetites."

The librarian didn't know the half of it, Maddy thought happily.

Scrutinizing the new bride's appearance, Ella said, "Doesn't look like you've missed too many meals lately either, girl. You've put on weight since the last time I saw you. Living here must agree with you."

Maddy hoped her face didn't look as red as it felt. Good grief, but the woman was blunt! "Ah, yes, you're exactly right. I have put on some weight, Ella. You know what the holidays are like. And I've been doing a great deal of baking and eating myself silly. Pete has a real sweet tooth, I've discovered." She hoped the woman bought the explanation. Ella Grady was too astute for her own good. And a notorious gossip, according to Allison.

The older woman patted her hand and smiled softly. "I just know you and Pete are going to be very happy together, Maddy. And I'm so glad you'll be staying on in Sweetheart. Everyone I've spoken to is excited at the prospect of you opening up your own business here.

"Though a few were surprised, myself included, that Pete was agreeable to it. That man has a stubborn streak in him a mile wide. I'm relieved he's relaxed his opinions somewhat. Things would have ended up quite differently, if he'd done so years ago."

"You're speaking of his late wife?"

Ella nodded. "Bethany was a lovely young woman, and her death, coming at that young an age, was such a tragedy. We never thought Pete would recover from it. He was so intent on Bethany having that baby." She shook her head. "But that's all water under the bridge. He has you now, and no doubt he's figured out that he's extremely lucky."

Maddy forced a smile, but she was starting to get a queasy feeling in the pit of her stomach that had nothing to do with her pregnancy.

JOHN WAS STARING into his champagne glass, lost in thought, and didn't see Allison approach from the opposite side of the room until she was standing right next to him.

Dressed in a red satin two-piece suit trimmed with rhinestone buttons, she looked like an angel, and the sight of her made John's heart beat faster, though he did his best to hide his emotions. He'd been hiding them for so long, he was getting pretty good at it.

"Hey, Ally! You did a good job as the maid of honor," he said, and the pretty blonde smiled.

"You know what they say, always a bridesmaid, never a bride."

John shrugged, taking a sip of his drink, not bothering to respond. He wasn't in the mood for Ally's marriage jokes tonight.

"What are you looking so glum about tonight, Dr. Taggart? This is a joyous occasion, or have you forgotten?"

He drew her to a quiet corner where they couldn't be overheard. "I'm worried that Pete's going to get hurt, Ally. He's just starting to recover from Bethany's death, and now I think he's in love with Maddy. If this marriage doesn't work out, it could destroy him."

"Excellent!" She grinned, then added quickly at his shocked expression, "I mean about Pete being in love with Maddy. You see, Maddy told me just this afternoon that she loves Pete, so there's really nothing for you to worry about.''

He arched a dark brow. "She did?"

"Yes. And you'd better not breathe a word of what I've just told you to your brother, or I'll never confide in you again. Let Pete and Maddy realize themselves what is so obvious to the rest of us, with the possible exception of you, Dr. Taggart."

Feeling inordinately relieved, he wrapped his arm about the woman's trim waist and gave a gentle squeeze. "Thanks for letting me know." The lemon scent of her hair tickled his senses, and he inhaled deeply.

"When are you going to make the trek down the aisle, Ally? You're not getting any younger, you know." And he had just the groom in mind—himself!

"Well, thank you very much!" She did her best to look affronted, but couldn't quite carry it off. She was grinning too widely. "And here I thought I looked like a million bucks in this new suit, which cost me almost that much, I might add."

"You know you look good. You always do. That's not what I meant."

"I'm not in any hurry to become some man's possession, John. I just got out from under my father's control, and I'm not anxious to give up my freedom again."

"Not all men are as controlling as your old man was."

She caressed his cheek. "That's why we're such good friends, John. You're nothing like Jason Montgomery.

"And you're forgetting something. If I get married, our relationship can't remain the same. It's doubtful my husband would approve of our spending so much time together."

Since he intended to be that husband, John didn't think that was going to prove a problem.

Chapter Eight

Maddy paced the confines of the bridal suite's large bathroom, the tile floor cold beneath her feet, and wondered if she'd made a big mistake.

As soon as the guests had departed, she'd hurried upstairs to get ready for her new husband, hoping to give herself some time to think before she had to face him, while Pete bid a final farewell to his brothers. They were both greatly indebted to Mark and John for all they had done to make the wedding a reality.

Allison's and Ella's comments had started her worrying, and she was fearful that Pete had misled her regarding his feelings toward her career.

Setting down her hairbrush, she gazed into the large gilt antique mirror above the sink. "Well, Maddy, there's just one thing left to do." She would talk to Pete, find out the truth of his feelings regarding her plan to resume her career, *before* consummating their marriage. It was the only sensible, rational thing she could think of, because if they didn't see eye to eye on something so important to her, there was no point in going forward.

But as she slipped the sheer black negligee over her head and it shimmied down her body, caressing her bare skin, as Pete's hands would caress her in just a few short minutes, she didn't feel very sensible.

What she felt was hot. Hot, tingly and eager to make love with her husband.

And she didn't think Pete was going to be at all rational once he got a good look at her in this getup.

The nightgown left nothing to the imagination, just as her friend had predicted. Her breasts and nipples were clearly visible beneath the sheer material, making her look like a woman with more on her mind than talk. The archaic term "hussy" came to mind. If The Sweetheart Inn had been a bordello, she would have felt right at home. Madam Maddy, Sweetheart's sweet tart.

"Good grief!" she whispered, eyes wide as she stared at her reflection. The man didn't stand a chance.

"Maddy, are you coming out of there anytime this century?"

Pete's voice floated in through the closed door, and she jerked, not realizing he'd come upstairs. Her heart started pounding loud in her chest, and she pressed her hand against it.

"I'm coming in after you, if you're not out here in ten seconds."

Sucking in a deep, fortifying breath, Maddy dabbed a few drops of perfume between her breasts and tried to remain focused on what she had to say as she floated out to meet her new husband.

Pete stood by the window, sipping from a glass of chilled champagne as he gazed out into the cold, starlit night. He was shirtless, and it was difficult not to drool at the sight of those well-developed pecs and bulging biceps. The way the tuxedo trousers cupped his sex gave Maddy plenty of indication as to what was on his mind.

"I'm sorry I took so long."

Pete turned at the sound of her voice, and his eyes lit with admiration and promise as he sucked in huge gulps of air. The provocative picture Maddy presented sent a punch straight to his gut, leaving him breathless and somewhat off-kilter. "Wow!" His eyes widened. "Where'd you get that?"

His reaction bolstered her courage and she pirouetted for him, feeling not at all self-conscious. "Do you like it? Allison picked it out."

"Allison Montgomery?" He shook his head in disbelief. Who would have ever guessed the ice princess had it in her? Certainly not him, but he supposed his younger brother knew. John had been sniffing after Allison for years.

"Hell, yes, I like it! I like it just fine."

"Is there enough champagne for me to join you?" she asked, hoping the alcohol would calm her nerves and buy her some time. She might not be a virgin, but this was still her wedding night.

Zeroing in on her large breasts and taut nipples, Pete licked his lips in anticipation, and his throat grew hoarse. "Ah, sure." Filling a crystal flute with the golden bubbly, he handed it to her. "You look absolutely beautiful, Maddy. I'm not sure I can wait much longer to make love to you."

The past few nights had been torture as he lay in the bedroom next to hers, listening to the soft mewling sounds she made in her sleep, hearing the distinctive creak of the bedsprings every time she turned over. He imagined her naked and waiting for him with a soft smile on her lips. And the result of those imaginings had been a succession of sleepless nights and cold showers in the morning.

Ask him, Maddy. Ask him about his true feelings.

But she couldn't. She didn't want to spoil the perfect moment. Not tonight. Not on her wedding night. Tomorrow would be soon enough to face reality once again, Maddy told herself.

Padding toward him on bare feet, she placed her hand against the soft furring on his chest and whispered, "I don't want to wait, either."

Removing the glass from her hand, he drew her closer, kissing her passionately, devouring her with his mouth, tongue, tasting all the sweetness that she offered. The kiss seemed to go on forever, until Pete finally pulled back, breathing hard as he tried to regain his equilibrium.

Maddy's kisses were like a narcotic, and he was fast becoming an addict; he had to have them.

"We won't have much of a wedding night, if we keep this up," he told her.

Boldly she reached down and cupped his sex. "Oh, I think you're *up* for it, Mr. Taggart."

With a low growl, Pete scooped Maddy into his arms and carried her to the king-size bed, depositing her in the center of it. "You're asking for it, woman!"

Smiling seductively, she said, "Indeed, I am. Now take your pants off real slow. I want you to give me the kind of peep show I just provided for you." Leaning back against the pillows, she waited, wondering if that heightened color on her husband's cheeks was a true blush or the result of too much champagne. She suspected it was a bit of both.

"I'm not entirely certain I can get this zipper down—" he smiled sheepishly "—due to a rather large problem."

Giggling, she scooted on her knees to the edge of the bed. "Shall I help?" Not waiting for him to answer, she moved forward, her fingers going to the crotch of his pants, and she caressed slowly, outlining the hard, long ridge of his erection, while tugging down the metal fastener carefully.

He gasped, and she smiled triumphantly, pleased she could affect him, excite him, as he did her. Freeing his sex, Maddy eased down his pants and tasted him, taking him into her mouth—something she had done for no other man before.

Pete groaned as if he were in physical pain. "Maddy! It'll all be over before it begins, if you don't stop what you're doing."

Like a siren, she held out her hand and beckoned

him to join her. "Come and make love to me, Pete.
I want you so badly."

Not needing to be asked twice, he covered her
body with his own, licking and sucking her swollen
nipples through the sheer material of her gown, then
removing the barrier completely to bare her body to
his view.

"You're so lovely. You make a man forget—"
He kissed her breasts, chin, cheeks, then finally settled on her luscious lips, while his hands moved up
and down her thighs in agonizing slowness—a promise of things yet to come.

Maddy tingled in places she never knew existed,
and the yearning, the heartfelt desire she felt for this
man, increased beyond boundaries.

He moved down her body, placing tender kisses
between her legs, and she squirmed restlessly, opening herself to him, needing the release that only he
could provide. When his mouth descended on her
and he tasted, plunging his tongue deep inside, she
thought she would die from the sheer pleasure of it.
"Pete!" she cried out on a breathless whisper.

"You're mine, Maddy. Never forget it. I've placed
my brand on you."

His possessive words were endearing and filled her
with tenderness. She caressed his cheek. "I won't,
because you're mine now, too. For better or worse."
To love and to cherish, till death us do part.

"Oh, baby! It's going to get a whole lot better,"
he promised, then slid her legs apart and entered her
quickly, pleased to find her small and tight. "You

feel so good." He moved slowly at first, allowing her to get used to his larger size, then increased the pace.

Like warm brandy, Maddy's blood surged hot through her veins, heating every inch of her. "Yes! Oh, my yes! That feels *so* good. Don't stop! Don't ever stop."

Lifting her buttocks, he plunged in to the hilt, and Maddy screamed as she attained her climax, Pete reaching his soon after.

"Maddy!" he said when he could breathe again. He'd never felt so complete, so totally satisfied before.

So in love?

"That was incredible! You were incredible." He brushed damp strands of hair away from her forehead and kissed her tenderly, cradling her to him.

Feelings he thought dead and buried rose to the surface. Like waves crashing against the shore, they threatened to drown him with their intensity, bringing a lump to his throat and an ache deep within his chest.

A soft smile crossed Maddy's lips, and her heart felt full to bursting she was so happy, so fulfilled. "I've never experienced anything quite so wonderful before."

And it was true.

Being in love made all the difference in the world. And she was most definitely in love.

They made love several more times during the night, and each time it was on the tip of Maddy's tongue to reveal her feelings for Pete. But she held back, hoping that someday he would grow to love her as much as she loved him.

She could wait, she vowed. Wait for eternity, if she had to.

THE FOLLOWING MORNING Maddy and Pete were in the truck with the heater turned on full blast, heading back to the ranch, when suddenly Pete took a detour off the main street onto Grant Avenue and pulled up in front of a two-story yellow house Maddy had never set eyes on before.

Before she could ask what was going on, her new husband shoved the gearshift into Park and cut the engine. "I called Dr. Peterson this morning while you were in the shower, Maddy," he confessed. "Doc's agreed to see you, to make sure everything is going well with the pregnancy."

"What?" Startled, she sat stiff backed against the seat, growing more incensed with every second that passed. "You called the doctor without consulting me first? I don't appreciate that, Pete. Not at all." Especially as sore as she felt this morning, she certainly didn't want some strange doctor poking and prodding her. And she certainly didn't like Pete's underhanded tactics. She wasn't a child. She didn't need to be told what to do.

"Laura Peterson is a very good doctor. And I thought since she's a woman that you wouldn't mind letting her take a look at you." He wasn't about to let anything happen to her now. Not after...

"I'm fine. I don't need—"

He reached for her hand, caressing each gloved finger. "Prenatal care is very important. And unless I miss my guess you haven't had any, right?"

She shook her head and sighed, knowing what he said was true, but disliking his tactics, nevertheless.

"You're almost three months along, Maddy. You need to begin taking vitamins. And you need to make certain that everything is okay with the baby." He placed his hand on her abdomen and rubbed gently. "I wouldn't want anything to happen to either one of you. Please do this for me."

She felt frustrated and manipulated, and didn't quite know what to do about it. Pete was her husband and he cared. That was something.

"All right. I'll see your Dr. Peterson." At least the doctor was a woman. It was some consolation. "But if you do something like this behind my back again, Pete Taggart, you won't like the consequences."

His lips twitched. "As I recall, I did something behind your back last night, and I didn't get so much as one complaint."

At the delicious memory, she socked him in the arm and thrust open the car door, eager to put distance between them.

"EVERYTHING LOOKS JUST fine, Mrs. Taggart," the doctor told her upon completion of the examination. "You're about twelve weeks along, as near as I can tell. An ultrasound would give us a better indication and could determine the sex of your child. But you'd have to go to Denver for that procedure. I'm not equipped here as yet to administer them."

"I don't think that's necessary," Maddy stated. There were few mysteries in life left. The sex of her unborn child was something she could anticipate, look forward to. She didn't want to know in advance, no matter if that made decorating the nursery easier.

Nursery! They needed a nursery for the baby.

"I'm giving you a prescription for some prenatal vitamins that contain folic acid. Make sure you take them every day. And here's a couple of books you can read about the changes your body is going through." She placed a small pile of books on the expectant mother's lap, then smiled ruefully.

"There's one here on the joys of childbirth, though you might not think it so joyful an experience when it actually occurs. I don't like to present my patients with a false picture. It won't be a walk in the park, especially if you decide to go the natural route, but I'll do my best to minimize your discomfort."

Natural childbirth! Maddy hadn't given that any consideration. Oh, there were so many things to think about, so many changes taking place.

She must have looked concerned, because the doctor patted her hand and said, "I hope I'm not overwhelming you with all of this, Maddy."

With her dark hair and soft brown eyes, Dr. Laura Peterson looked too young, and way too attractive to be a doctor. But she was as skillful as any Maddy had met in New York and had a far better bedside manner, for which Maddy was grateful. "You're not.

And thank you, Dr. Peterson, for seeing me on such short notice. And on New Year's Day, of all things. I must apologize for interrupting your holiday. I'm afraid once Pete gets something in his head—''

Laura Peterson smiled in understanding, giving her knee a pat. "All expectant fathers turn into worry-warts, Maddy. Your husband's behavior is nothing new. And it's probably going to get much worse before it gets better, so be prepared."

That's exactly what worried Maddy, though she kept those fears to herself.

Pete was pacing the empty waiting room when she emerged a few minutes later. "The doctor has pronounced me healthy as a horse," she told him, and his face lit with a relieved smile. "You can quit worrying about this baby now."

"Has Dr. Laura given you a due date?"

Maddy nodded. "Around the end of July, beginning of August, give or take a week. New babies are unpredictable."

As unpredictable as new husbands, apparently.

WHEN THEY ARRIVED back at the ranch, Pete insisted on carrying Maddy over the threshold, despite Rufus's constant barks of disapproval. Then he proceeded to carry her up the stairs in Rhett Butler fashion to his—their—room, where he declared with a teasing grin, "I've always been a firm believer in starting the New Year off with a bang."

It was one resolution Maddy was eager and willing to accept.

Millie Criswell

Chapter Nine

Meltdown. That's what Maddy was feeling at the moment. Having spent another blissful night in her husband's arms—they'd made love every morning and night since the wedding ceremony two weeks ago—her body felt deliciously melted, like hot fudge pouring over vanilla ice cream, only sweeter.

The snow had melted, too. As quickly as it had come, the snow was now melting from the increased temperature and succession of sunny days. The weather forecasters blamed it on El Niño or La Niña, she forgot which one. Maddy was just happy to see the end of the inclement weather. At least, for the time being. Pete said the weather in Colorado was contrary and unforgiving, so it was likely they'd have more snow before all was said and done.

Staring out the upstairs bedroom window, Maddy observed her husband on the back of Junebug, his favorite mare. He was giving the buckskin and several of the horses some much needed exercise. Someday, when she learned to ride and wasn't pregnant, she'd be able to help him. But for now, Maddy was content to watch him put the horses through their paces.

There was something to be said for a man in tight-fitting jeans, cowboy boots and a black Stetson. "Ride 'em cowboy" had taken on a whole new meaning, she realized, smiling to herself.

Watching Pete work the horses was far more agreeable than the task awaiting her, Maddy thought, gazing down at the big packing boxes that had arrived last evening via the parcel service. She heaved a dispirited sigh. Sorting through all her pretty clothes—items she could no longer wear at the moment—was sure to depress her.

Her former secretary, Liz Gordon, had volunteered—bless her heart!—to pack up Maddy's apartment and ship her clothing and other personal items to her when Maddy had called to inform the woman, and the powers that be, that she would not be coming back.

The furniture, small appliances and such, Liz would arrange to store, until such time as Maddy figured out what to do with them. The modern design of her furniture would not complement the Taggart antiques. Most likely, she would ask Liz to sell them or donate the goods to the Salvation Army or Goodwill.

As Maddy had predicted, Lassiter, Owens and Cumberland had been only too happy to accept her resignation. They'd cut her a generous severance check, with an added bonus for her work on the Singleton brokerage account, and even given her a glowing letter of recommendation, should she decide to seek employment elsewhere. Anywhere but there would make them inordinately happy.

That was especially true in David's case, who had not seen fit to write a note or wish her well. Good riddance! she thought. She'd found herself a real man, not an empty suit.

Maddy took one look at the small closet and another at the large cartons and knew immediately that something had to give. There wouldn't be room in Pete's closet for all of her apparel. Admittedly, she had a lot. Clothes and shoes were her passion. And when she added the maternity clothes that she intended to buy this afternoon when she and Allison went shopping…well, there was just no way it was all going to fit.

The clothes she'd been wearing had reached far beyond uncomfortable, and Maddy knew it was time to bite the bullet and expand her horizons, and her waistbands. Jeans were no longer an option. She couldn't get the zipper up.

Which was why she was happy that Allison knew of a charming boutique that had recently opened downtown and had volunteered to take Maddy in her four-wheel drive to visit A Pea In The Pod this afternoon. She was looking forward to the excursion, and to being with her new friend again.

Woman could not live on sex alone. Her brain, she thought with a naughty smile, needed stimulation, too.

Tapping her fingernail against her cheek, she gazed at the mess of clothes again and came to a decision. She would purchase one of those huge antique wardrobes to increase their closet space. Until then, the clothes would have to remain in the boxes. She couldn't wear them anyway. Caressing the Italian pump reverently, she tossed it back into the carton and heaved a sigh. High heels and pregnant women were not a good match.

Removing her green silk robe—last year's birthday present from her sister—Maddy stared critically at her naked body in the full-length cheval mirror and made a face of disgust. For once she had big boobs, and she couldn't even enjoy the fact, because everything else was big, too.

She'd read all of the books Dr. Peterson had given her, but they hadn't prepared her for looking like a cow. Though Pete kept insisting she was beautiful, she still felt fat and unattractive. And besides, Pete wasn't totally unbiased: he was a rancher and liked cows, she reminded herself.

"Is this a private show, or can anyone attend?" Pete asked from the doorway. He stood grinning, arms crossed over his broad chest, drawing a startled gasp from Maddy.

"You scared me half to death! Don't you ever sneak up on me like that again, Pete Taggart."

He came up behind her and wrapped his large hands around her middle, placing his palms on her abdomen. "How's my baby doing today?" he asked, kissing the back of her neck and bringing forth goosebumps, making her forget that she was supposed to be annoyed with him.

"Which one?"

He cupped her breasts, and her nipples hardened instantly. "Oh, baby, baby," he whispered, rolling her nipples between his fingers as their searing gazes caught in the mirror.

Maddy bit the inside of her cheek, trying to remain unaffected, which was next to impossible. "You have a one-track mind, Mr. Taggart." Unfortunately, it was on the same track as her own.

His hand moved down to caress the soft, damp curls between her thighs, and she moaned as his clever fingers explored, teased and excited. "I can't get enough of you, woman. You've bewitched me."

She turned in his arms and kissed his chin. "It's the quilt, cowboy. I told you it had magical powers."

He laughed, then kissed her soundly. "You, Mrs. Taggart, have a vivid imagination. And if I wasn't expecting my brother to come over at any moment, I'd—"

"John's coming over?" Her eyes widened, and she stepped back out of his embrace, reaching for her robe. "Did he say why?"

Her interest in his brother's visit made Pete frown, and his eyes narrow in suspicion. "Yeah. He's coming over to check out a couple of the horses for me. Why? You anxious to see the handsome doctor again?" His smile didn't quite reach his eyes.

Maddy shot him a look of disapproval that told him he wasn't fooling anyone. "Yes, but not for the reasons you think, so quit being jealous." Though she was secretly delighted he was, and took hope in the fact that maybe he loved her just a little bit. Jealousy was a powerful emotion, which meant Pete could have stronger feelings for her than he admitted to himself.

Unless, of course, it really was the quilt behind his emotions.

"John's asked me to help him form an advertising campaign for his business," she explained. "He's one of my very first clients, along with Mark, of course. The Sweetheart Inn has retained my services as well."

"Do you mind telling me what the hell you're talking about, woman? I'm missing something here." John and Mark had retained her services? Over his dead body. Wait till he got his hands on those brothers of his. He didn't want Maddy spending time with anyone but him.

"I'm bringing my advertising expertise to the good folks in Sweetheart. I'll be opening up my own business, as soon as I can find the proper location, and—"

"Whoa!" He held up his hands, looking dazed by her admission. "Are you talking about running a business in town? A business you'd have to drive to?"

"Of course." Her brow wrinkled in confusion. "We've discussed this, Pete. Don't you remember?"

"I remember we talked about you working part-time, here at the ranch. Not driving into town each and every day. You're pregnant, Maddy! You should be slowing down, resting and taking care of yourself, not thinking about opening up a business. There's plenty of time for that after the baby is born.'' By then, he could convince her not to act on the idea. Pete could be very persuasive when he put his mind to it.

Maddy's chin shot up defiantly. ''There's no time like the present, in my opinion. In fact, I may check out some real estate possibilities this afternoon. Allison and I are going shopping for maternity clothes, and I—''

''Allison! Is she planning to drive? Because I don't like the way that woman drives. She's a menace on the road, and it wouldn't be safe for you to be in the same car with her. Though the roads are passable, they're loaded with potholes.''

At first, Pete's words angered Maddy, but then she saw the genuine fear in his eyes—fear that he might lose another wife and child—and she took a deep breath and wrapped her arms about his waist. ''You mustn't worry about me, Pete. Allison's an excellent driver.'' At least she hoped so. ''And as soon as I open up an account at the bank and deposit my paycheck and bonus, I intend to buy a car of my own and drive myself, so stop being so silly and overprotective about all of this.''

''But—''

She placed her fingertips over his lips. ''I realize you think you have reason to worry, because of what happened to Beth, but nothing like that is going to happen to me or the baby. I promise.''

Resting his chin on the top of her head, he held her close. "I wish I could believe that.''

"Believe it,'' she whispered, then brought his head down and kissed him, trying to convey all that was in her heart without uttering a word.

The kiss had the predictable effect, and soon they were rolling about on the bed, kissing and fondling like a couple of sex-starved teenagers, and forgetting all about businesses and visitors, until the front door banged shut loudly and Rufus began to bark.

"Hell,'' Pete said, looking at Maddy's warm and willing body with no small amount of dismay, then reaching for his pants. "I forgot all about John.''

Maddy smiled seductively. "Should I take that as a compliment?''

"We'll talk about this car and driving business later, Maddy. I've got to get downstairs now.''

Her lips formed a pout. "Too bad. I just thought of a hundred more persuasive ways to take your mind off things. Are you sure you don't want me to show you?''

At the prominent bulge forming between his legs, she laughed. "Dammit, Maddy! This is not funny. John's going to— Never mind. It's just not funny.''

But Maddy thought it was and she broke into fits of giggles as soon as her husband shut the door behind him.

She and Pete were likely to disagree on many things, including her working in town, but making up after the arguments was going to be highly entertaining.

"I JUST LOVE ALL THE NEW clothes you bought," Allison told her companion, clutching one of Maddy's shopping bags. "Especially that green pantsuit with the lemon-yellow silk top. Will you let me borrow it when I get pregnant?"

Maddy smiled indulgently. Her friend was enamored of all things having to do with babies.

They had just left the maternity shop, where Maddy had splurged on several casual outfits, two special-occasion dresses and a ton of underwear—the new bras would be especially welcome—and were walking down Main Street toward the library. Allison had told her Ella Grady had asked to see her, though Maddy had no idea why.

Hopefully, she hadn't heard about her pregnancy yet. She was hoping to keep her secret about the baby a while longer yet, though she knew how fast news traveled in a town the size of Sweetheart.

"Of course you can borrow it," she finally replied with a teasing twinkle in her eye. "Will that be anytime soon?"

Allison shrugged. "Who knows? I don't have a sperm donor yet." Then she grinned. "Guess I could go to Denver and buy some frozen stuff, but that doesn't seem all that appealing."

Laughing, Maddy said, "Well, it's definitely not as much fun as doing it the old-fashioned way."

"I take it Pete's good in the sack?" Allison's

brows rose inquisitively, making Maddy blush to the tips of her toes.

"I have no intention of discussing my sex life with you, Allison Montgomery, but you can take it from me that all the Taggart men seem to be highly capable of pleasing a woman. I think it's in their genes."

Pete had told her stories about his Taggart ancestors that could give romance novels a run for their money, and judging by her husband's skill in bed, she was sure they were accurate accounts.

Allison's expression grew thoughtful as she mulled over Maddy's words. "I kissed John once in junior high school," she confessed. "He had very soft lips, as I recall." She couldn't quite disguise the sigh that escaped her lips.

"Well, there you go."

The blonde shook her head, looking at Maddy as if she'd lost her mind. "John and I are friends, and friends are hard to come by. I wouldn't jeopardize our relationship for anything."

Hearing how adamant the woman was, Maddy thought it wise to let the matter drop. John would have to be the one to convince her otherwise. "Did Ella say what she wanted to talk to me about?" she asked as they headed up the front steps of the library.

Sweetheart's lending library was a two-story brick building with three large white columns supporting a wide front portico. It reminded Maddy of an antebellum mansion. "What a lovely building. It must be quite historic."

"Yes, it's almost as old as Ella," Allison quipped with a grin. "Come on." She tugged Maddy's hand. "Ella will have our hides if we're late. She's a stickler for punctuality." When they reached the door, Allison paused, placing her hand on Maddy's arm.

"Ella's motive in wanting to see you today is probably to rope you into helping out with Sweetheart's annual Valentine's Day dance. I thought it only fair to give you a heads-up, in case you want to come up with an excuse. Ella's always in charge of the dance committee, and she's always looking for victims…er…volunteers."

"But that sounds like fun. How come you're not more enthused? Don't you like going?" Maddy hadn't attended a dance since high school, and she loved to dance.

Her friend shrugged as she opened the door leading into the library and immediately lowered her voice to a whisper. Years of being scolded by Ella had finally sunk in. "I love the dance. It's something the whole town looks forward to every year. But Ella's a slave driver. John and I worked on her committee last year, and she drove us nuts."

"I can hardly believe that sweet old woman could drive anyone insane."

Allison smiled at her friend's naiveté. "Don't say I didn't warn you."

There was no time to question her further, because Ella, dressed in a peacock-blue polyester pantsuit and a pair of white tennis shoes, was marching down the hallway toward them, looking at her wristwatch and shaking her head in disapproval.

"Goodness, whatever has kept you two? I thought we agreed on two o'clock, Allison."

"It's my fault, Ella," Maddy said by way of explanation as they followed the older woman down the dimly lit hall to her office at the rear of the building. The musty scent of old books rose up to greet her, making her feel slightly nauseous. Tuna had not been a good choice for lunch.

"I was doing some shopping and the time just got away from me, I'm afraid."

"Well, now that you're finally here, I was hoping to convince you to help out with our annual library fund-raiser. It's a very worthwhile and important event. And the proceeds are used to purchase new books for the library, as well as computers."

When they were finally seated in Ella's office, Allison shot Maddy an I-told-you-so look.

"I know you're probably busy, starting that new business and all, but we could really use someone with your advertising experience. I was hoping you could do up some posters, make a few flyers, that sort of thing."

Pete was not going to like this, was Maddy's first thought, right before she smiled and said, "Of course, Pete and I would be only too happy to help."

Allison merely rolled her eyes.

"WHY ON EARTH did you let Ella rope you into working on that fund-raiser?" Pete wanted to know, draining the pasta into the colander over the sink before placing it in a large ceramic bowl. He'd cooked dinner tonight as a surprise for Maddy, but the surprise was really on him.

"It's even worse than that. I volunteered both of us. Ella needs help with the decorating and lighting, and I told her how handy you were with electrical things."

He paled. "Oh hell!" The last time he'd worked on the dance committee, Florence Leechman had made a pass at him. No matter that he'd been married at the time. His former high school classmate had tried to stick her tongue down his throat while he was lying flat on his back working beneath the stage on the wiring. The memory still had the power to make him shiver, not to mention gag!

"Don't worry. John and Allison are helping, too. And Mark's been coerced into cooking some of the refreshments. Feel better?" She grinned at his sullen attitude, then sampled the spaghetti. The sauce was from a jar but still very tasty.

"This is good! I'm sorry you had to cook tonight, Pete. I didn't know my meeting with Ella was going to take so long. And then Allison and I stopped by Ed's Motor World to look at cars."

He paled even whiter this time. "Cars? You stopped to look at cars, without me?"

"Well, you didn't seem very interested when I told you I wanted to buy one, and—"

He set down his fork, his expression determined. "We'll go first thing tomorrow. I don't want you coming home with some teeny, impractical sports car.''

Her face fell. "I was actually looking at the new BMW. It's so cute, and Ed says it goes like a 'bat outta hell,' to quote him.''

"Ed Bixby is a jackass. He flunked auto mechanics, for chrissake! Which is precisely the reason I'm going with you tomorrow. We'll find something sensibly priced and suitable for—'' He was about to say "a wife and mother,'' but thought better of it. Maddy was likely to bash him over the head if he did.

"I don't wish to be rude, Peter, but it is my money that I'm planning to spend, and if I want to buy an outrageously expensive, sexy sports car, then I will.''

"And that's another thing. I'm perfectly capable of supporting you. There's no need for you to be spending your own money.''

She rolled her eyes. "Oh, quit being so archaic. I just got a bonus of $350,000. I think I can afford to make a contribution to this marriage, don't you?''

Pete's eyes widened even as he frowned, but he didn't argue further with her. He just kept on eating, which was no guarantee at all that Maddy was going to get her own way. Her husband, she'd found out, was what psychologists called a passive-aggressive personality. Somehow he always got his way without putting up a fight.

Well, not this time, she vowed. She had her eye on that sleek, silver BMW and she intended to buy it.

ED BIXBY WAS A WALKING CLICHÉ in his white patent leather shoes, brown-and-yellow-checked pants, and a camel hair sportcoat that had seen better days. Maddy, however, didn't find him nearly as distasteful as her husband did, for Ed had taken her side in the debate over the shiny BMW.

"It's a good investment, Pete. And just think of the fun you and the missus will have driving it." He smiled a too-wide smile, exposing all of his gums.

"Congratulations, by the way! Didn't know you'd gone and gotten hitched again. And to such a looker."

Pete didn't bother to disguise his disgust. "You'd sell a blind man a stick shift without batting an eye, Bixby, so don't go giving me the hard sell. We're not interested in the BMW. What else you got?"

"Now wait a minute, Pete!" Maddy protested, clutching her husband's arm. "I don't think I've made that final decision yet."

He smiled sweetly at her. "Let's just see what else Ed has to show us, babe." When Ed walked farther ahead, he whispered, "Never show your hand too early, Maddy. We won't get a good deal if you do."

Appeased for the moment, she nodded, then followed the men to the back lot where the used cars were held. "I may as well tell you right now, Pete," Maddy said, pulling up short, "that I am not buying a used car, so there is no point in looking at what appear to be junk heaps."

"Now, Maddy..."

"Don't 'now Maddy' me, Pete Taggart. I'm not

doing it. I worked too hard for my money, and—''
She shook her head, turned on her heel and walked
back the way she had come.

Heaving a sigh of exasperation at his wife's stubborn, independent streak, Pete removed his hat,
plowing his fingers through his hair. Then he said to
Ed, ''What do you have new in SUVs? I want something big and safe. A Sherman tank with style, if you
get my drift.''

The salesman smiled smoothly…oily, in Pete's
opinion. ''I've got just what you want. In fact, your
wife is walking in the right direction. We just got in
some new Explorers and Expeditions and a honey of
a Suburban. I'll cut you a terrific deal. Tell you what,
I'll even throw in floor mats.''

An hour later, after much haggling and negotiating
on Pete's part—he got the floor mats and a whole lot
more—Maddy held the keys to a brand-new candy-
apple-red Ford Expedition, and she didn't look at all
happy about it.

''It's huge and not at all attractive,'' she told him.
''I'll never be able to park the stupid thing. Why
can't I buy the sports car? It's small and manageable.
And quite adorable.''

''And where will you put the baby seat, Maddy?
The stroller? The car bed? Diaper bag? Groceries?
The laundry and such? Did you see the trunk of the
Beemer? It barely held the spare tire.''

''If it's good enough for James Bond, I don't see
why it wouldn't be good enough for me.''

Pete didn't bother to point out that 007 didn't carry

his Walther PPK in a diaper bag. "Trust me. I know a lot more about this sort of thing than you do." That statement had Maddy's eyes narrowing. "The Expedition is going to be a great car for you. And safe. Did you see the *Consumer Reports* rating on the vehicle? That's important, you know."

"Only if I intend to ram large buildings, which I don't. The air bag alone will probably kill me." He paled suddenly, and Maddy clasped his arm, instantly apologetic. "I'm sorry, Pete. I forgot. I shouldn't have said something so insensitive."

He shrugged. "It's all right. Look, I know I'm being overly cautious, but if you insist on driving yourself, then I'd feel better if you were driving with some metal around you. And don't forget—this has four-wheel drive."

Only a man would find that a bonus. "I don't intend to go off road."

"And when it snows, what about then?"

Maddy gazed longingly at the silver BMW and heaved a disappointed sigh. "I hate it that you're practical."

He buckled her into the seat and new car smell surrounded her. At least the seats were leather, that was something. And they were heated. Another bonus. And it did have a CD player with Dolby. "Rufus will like it, I guess."

He leaned in through the open car door and kissed her. "Thanks for humoring me. Now drive carefully. I'll be following right behind in the pickup. If you have any trouble at all, just flash your headlights and pull over.''

"It's good thing you're so cute, Pete Taggart, or else I'd be mad as hell at you.''

"Don't be mad at me, sweetheart. I'm only thinking about your welfare and the baby's. And...and well, I love you.''

Chapter Ten

"Wait, Pete! What did you say?" Maddy yelled, but he had already slammed the door shut and was walk-ing back to his truck, leaving her staring wide-eyed and openmouthed after him. As hard as she tried, she couldn't get the window or the damn door to open. Apparently, neither worked without the engine run-ning. She hated her new car already.

Maddy was a tangle of nerves the entire way home. It wasn't bad enough that she was driving a strange vehicle that had the dimensions of a Mack truck, but her husband had just dropped a bombshell in her lap and then blithely walked away, as if telling her he loved her was an everyday occurrence.

Pete loved her! She smiled happily, feeling giddy at the thought as she gazed into the rearview mirror to see him following behind. She heaved a sigh of pure contentment. Pete had said he loved her.

And then she frowned. The quilt! It had to be the quilt that had caused the declaration. Pete had made it quite clear before they were married that he would never love again. So why should she believe anything had changed? It had to be the quilt, she decided, despondency replacing the jubilation of moments before.

Lost in thought as she pulled onto the muddy road leading to the ranch house, Maddy turned too sharply and smashed into the rural mailbox, taking it out completely.

She hit the brake, gazed in the rearview mirror to see her husband's displeased expression, then reversed, put the vehicle back into Drive, and continued on. "It's your own fault, Pete Taggart," she declared. "I told you this stupid car was too big."

Once she reached the house, she fairly vaulted from the car and dashed to the porch, unmindful of the puddle of slush she'd just stepped into, until the wet seeped through the soles of her shoes and stockings. Kicking off her shoes, and with a terse hello and wave to Rufus, who was barking happily in greeting, she ran up the stairs, pulling off her socks as she went.

As soon as she entered the guest room, Maddy made a beeline for the trunk, where she'd placed the quilt legend for safekeeping. Carefully removing it, she started to read, and her heart sank.

It was just as she thought. Pete's love for her had been foretold. The quilt had worked its magic, and now he was hopelessly in love with her because of some ridiculous spell conjured up all those years ago.

What should have been a momentous moment turned sour, and tears slipped down her cheeks. She didn't want Pete to love her because of some stupid legend. She wanted him to love her because he couldn't live without her, because she was the most important thing in his life.

But she knew that wasn't true.

Her hand went to her swollen belly. The baby was the most important thing in Pete's life. It was what had prompted his marriage proposal, with a little help from the quilt legend. She couldn't forget that the legend had played a large role in her recent marriage.

"Place this quilt upon your bed and in one month you shall be wed..."

And she had been, just as the legend foretold. Wedded and deliciously bedded.

"A kiss on the lips, the bargain will seal, and undying love will the couple soon feel."

Well, there it was. Proof positive in black and white. Pete loved her only because of the legend and the fact that they had kissed, sealing the bargain and their fate.

With a sigh, and feeling about as dejected as a body could feel, Maddy dropped onto the rocker and cradled her head, rocking back and forth.

It was how Pete found her a few minutes later.

"Maddy," he said, coming to kneel before her and grasping her hands. They were cold and he rubbed them between his to get the blood circulating. "What's wrong?" The tears in her eyes as she gazed up at him burned right into his gut, like acid eating into metal. "Don't cry, sweetheart. We can replace the mailbox. And the car's hardly been scratched."

He swallowed, thinking of the dent in the right front fender and felt slightly nauseated. "I'm not mad about it."

She swiped at her tears with the back of her hand. "I don't care about the mailbox, or the car, for that matter," she said, sniffing. "Back there at the car lot you said you loved me, but I know it's not true." She held out the wrinkled piece of parchment to him. "It's the quilt legend. It's worked its magic on you and now you think you're in love with me. And you're really not."

Pete heaved a sigh, wishing she had never found that damn legend of his great-grandma Maggie's; he felt like ripping it to shreds. For Maddy to think he didn't love her, didn't cherish her above all else, was just plain ridiculous. He loved her so much that he didn't know how he had existed before she came into his life.

"Maddy, stop being foolish. Of course, I love you. I'd never say such a thing if it wasn't true." It had taken him a while to finally admit it, being the stubborn fool that he was, but now he'd never been more sure of anything in his life.

"You told me you'd never fall in love again, Pete. I know you only married me because of the baby."

His words were being thrown back at him, biting him right in the ass. "I may have stupidly thought that at the time," he tried to explain, "but now I feel differently. I do love you. Please believe me, Maddy. I love you so very much."

"But you wouldn't have married me if it hadn't been for the baby. Isn't that true?"

Taking a deep breath, he squeezed her hand, unsure of how to answer. He opted for honesty. "Hell, I don't know, Maddy. Maybe. I mean—you were all alone and pregnant, and it seemed like the right thing to do."

She started crying again, harder this time. "So... so now I'm...I'm just a...a charity case, is that what you're saying?"

Hell and damnation, but the woman was putting words in his mouth. Pulling her forward into his lap, he brushed the hair away from her face. "Haven't I shown you with every kiss and caress how much I adore you? We've made love countless times, in every imaginable way possible. Can't you tell how I feel when I'm deep inside you?"

She shook her head. "Making love, having sex, is just something men are prone to do. It's part of your male chemical makeup. It doesn't have to mean anything. You forget, I know that firsthand."

At the unpleasant reminder, Pete forced down his anger. "Just because that bastard took advantage of you and left you high and dry is no reason to think that I'm just in this for the sex.

"It may be true that I hadn't had sex for four years before you came along, but—"

Her eyes widened at the admission. "Well, that just proves why you've been as randy as a goat," she wailed, burying her head in his chest, listening to his steady heartbeat. "You were sex starved, and I was available."

"I think you're blowing this whole thing out of proportion. I realize that pregnant women are often irrational and have hormone issues—"

Her eyes flashed green fire. "Don't go blaming this on my hormones! I hate it when people do that. I'm not irrational. I've loved you from the first moment I laid eyes on you. Well, maybe not the first. You were terribly rude. But I'm sure it was before I slept under that stupid quilt.

"But you—" She flailed her arms at him. "You just come up with this crazy idea that you're in love with me, then blurt it out, and, and—well, we both know that just isn't true."

Maddy's admission that she loved him filled Pete with such joy and jubilation that he wanted to shout out his feelings from the rooftop, to tell the world how much he loved Maddy and that she loved him. But, of course, he couldn't, because his stubborn wife had gone from angry to crying again.

"Please stop crying, sweetheart. You'll make yourself sick. If it makes you feel better, I'll retract the statement."

"Oh! It's just like a man to take back his declaration. You're all so fickle." She pushed out of his embrace and rose to her feet.

"I'm going downstairs to eat a quart of ice cream, and I don't care if it makes me as fat as a cow."

He smiled at the absurdity of her statement. "You're beautiful, Maddy. Nothing will ever change that. And I'll always love you, no matter how big and fat you get. I promise.''

Maddy kicked him in the shin with her bare foot, yelped when it hurt, then quit the room, leaving Pete confused, and more in love with her than ever.

THE FOLLOWING MORNING Maddy sat at the large dining room table, her art supplies and poster board spread out before her, trying to come up with a few catchy ideas for Sweetheart's Valentine's Day dance posters. The problem was she didn't feel very romantic.

For the first time since their wedding night, she and Pete hadn't made love, either last night or this morning. She felt bereft. And miserable. Because she knew it was all her fault for being so—she hated to admit it—irrational.

She drew a large picture of a cupid poised to shoot his arrow, then scribbled over it. How trite and amateurish! She had lost her creative abilities. She would have to tell Ella that she couldn't help out with the dance after all. The woman would be disappointed, but she'd get over it. Women were always getting over disappointment.

Didn't she know it?

"What're you doing?"

Pete strolled into the room with a cup of hot coffee and sat down next to her, and her heart gave a funny little surge at the sight of him. She'd purposely left their bed before he'd awakened, so as not to be tempted to make love with him, and she missed sharing the intimacy of their joining, of their talking together and making plans for the coming day.

"Are you working on the Valentine's Day dance project?" he asked, looking at her drawing, and her frown deepened.

"I'm fresh out of romantic ideas. I won't be able to do it. I'm going to call Ella and tell her to find someone else. That'll probably make you happy, right?"

Without replying, he reached into his pants' pocket and extracted a small box. "I was going to surprise you with this on Valentine's Day, but maybe it'd be better to give it to you now. It might inspire you."

Eyes wide with curiosity, she set down her charcoal, wiped her hands on her pants and took the box he proffered, trying to squelch down the pleasure she felt at the gesture, but she couldn't keep the excitement out of her voice when she asked, "What is it?"

"Just a little something I saw in town the other day when I went in for feed and decided you needed to have."

"But I don't really need anything, Pete. I—" She opened the lid and stopped midsentence, eyes widening.

Nestled in a bed of red satin was the most exquisite heart of diamonds. "Oh, Pete!" Her eyes filled with tears. "It's beautiful. But I can't accept it." She tried to hand it back to him, but he refused to take it. "Not after I was so horrible to you. It wouldn't be right."

He couldn't help grinning. Maddy always made

him smile. He hoped that would never change. "I'm a big boy, sweetheart. I can take it. Now lean this way so I can fasten the silver chain." When he had accomplished his task, he kissed her nape, making the tiny hairs stand up on end. "There. Now you truly have my heart."

"Oh, Pete!" Twisting about in her chair, she wrapped her arms about his neck and kissed him. "Thank you! I love it, and you. Even if I don't deserve it."

I love you, Maddy, he wanted to say, but was fearful of upsetting her again. So he kissed the top of her head and rose to his feet.

"I've got to drive into town to help Mark. The transmission blew on his truck, and he needs help with the repair. Do you want to come with me, or will you be okay here by yourself?"

She followed him into the front hallway. "Take the tank," she suggested, retrieving the keys from the hall table and dropping them into his outstretched hand. She didn't miss the spark of pure excitement in his eyes. Boys and their toys, she thought with a smile.

"I'll be fine here at home. I've got plenty of work to keep me busy, and Rufus to keep me company. Isn't that right, boy?" The dog barked, and she grinned. "See that? He's up for the job."

Pete shrugged into his leather bomber jacket. "You've decided to finish the poster, then?"

She tugged at the tiny heart around her throat. "I feel suddenly inspired."

"I'll be home in time for dinner."

"Dinner!" Her face flushed with embarrassment, her hands rising to cup her cheeks. "Oh no! I completely forgot. Allison invited us over to her house for dinner tonight, along with your brother. She thought the four of us could work on the musical selections for the dance. I've already accepted. I'm sorry."

"Not a problem. I'll be home in plenty of time." He drew her into his arms and kissed her, long and leisurely, then said, "Maybe that'll give you some additional inspiration."

With a wink, he disappeared out the door, leaving Maddy in a state of frustration, but definitely inspired.

"THE BEEF STROGANOFF WAS absolutely delicious, Allison. Thanks for inviting us. This is our first official meal out as a married couple, you know." Maddy smiled warmly at her friend, grateful Allison had come into her life. "I'm glad we got to share it with you and John."

"Hear, hear," John said, winking at his new sister-in-law. "You're sure a welcome addition to the family, Maddy. And much prettier to look at than either one of my brothers."

Maddy blushed at the compliment, while Pete frowned.

"A toast then. To Pete and Maddy," Allison said, raising her glass of merlot, waiting while the others followed suit—except Maddy, whose glass was filled with milk. "May you both be blessed with love and happiness, and many, many babies."

"I think one baby's enough for the time being."

"For the time being," Pete agreed. "But I'd like to have at least five or six."

Maddy nearly choked and set down her glass. "Are you serious? Five or six children isn't a responsible idea in this day and age, Pete. The population is already overburdened. Don't you agree, John?" She looked to her brother-in-law for confirmation.

The vet glanced down the opposite end of the table at his brother's irritated expression and grinned. It was obvious that Pete wasn't happy that his new wife had chosen *him* to back her up. "Well, I guess that depends on whether Pete is thinking about forming his own baseball team."

"All right, three then," Pete conceded. "But no less than three. And I want them all to look like Maddy."

"Pete'll keep you barefoot and pregnant, if you let him," Allison told her friend, and Maddy rolled her eyes. "Sounds to me like you two lovebirds should be left alone for a while. Come on, John. Let's go into the kitchen and get the dessert."

While John retrieved the plates from the cupboard, Allison fetched from the refrigerator the strawberry-glazed cheesecake she had prepared that morning and began to slice it into pieces.

"I guess you can see with your own two eyes that your brother and Maddy are truly in love," she told

John, keeping her voice purposely low, so the new-lyweds couldn't hear her. "Did you see the way they looked at each other? Whew!" She fanned herself. "The temperature must have risen fifty degrees."

"Maybe you were getting hot because you were sitting next to me," John retorted. "Did you ever consider that?" Ignoring the woman's shocked expression, he grabbed the plates and forks from the counter and hurried back into the living room, allowing Allison a little food for thought.

Pete and Maddy were looking at Ally's CD collection when John arrived, arguing over some of the songs that should be played at the dance.

"I think slow songs would be the best," Maddy advised. "The theme of the dance is going to be Let Me Call You Sweetheart, so I think the music should reflect a kind of old-fashioned romanticism."

Pete made a face. "You mean old fogy music. I'd rather get down and dirty. Arrowsmith, the Stones—"

"The standards are not old fogy music, Pete. How can you call Frank Sinatra's rendition of 'It Had to Be You' an old fogy song? It's a classic. And so terribly romantic."

John nodded in agreement. "One of my favorites, bro. Let's put it on and try it out. Shall we?"

When the soft, dreamy music floated out of the stereo, Pete drew Maddy into his arms. "You sure do smell good."

"You're supposed to be concentrating on the music, not on how I smell.'' She smiled up at him. ''But thank you.''

''I'd rather concentrate on you, sweetheart, because,'' he twirled her around, ''''it had to be you, wonderful you...''' he sang into her ear, pulling her closer.

''One of these days, Maddy, you're going to believe how madly in love I am with you, then you'll feel silly for having doubted me.''

She wanted to believe him. If only she could. But some perverse part of her couldn't allow for the possibility, couldn't let her believe that she was all that lovable. ''Pete, I—''

''Shh! Just let me hold you and enjoy the moment. We've got the rest of our lives to work out the rest.''

Maddy sighed at the glorious thought and kissed her husband on the lips.

Across the room, John approached Allison, who was sitting on the sofa, staring all moony eyed at the dancing couple, a million miles away in her thoughts. ''Would you like to dance, Ally?''

''No!'' She shook her head, then realizing she might have hurt John's feelings by her abruptness, amended, ''No, thank you.'' She pasted on a smile, wondering why the teasing comments he'd made in the kitchen bothered her so. ''I'm fine just where I am.''

He filled her glass with more wine and joined her on the sofa. ''It's nice to see my brother so happy. I never thought I'd live to see the day. Marriage agrees with him, I think.''

"Why don't you get married, John?" she asked, sipping on her wine. "You seem ready to settle down. And now that your veterinary clinic is doing so well, it seems the perfect time for you to find someone, get married and have kids." Though she knew if he did, she would lose her best friend. The thought did not sit well, and she frowned without realizing it.

John smiled inwardly. "You know, Ally, I've been giving that subject a lot of thought lately. Seeing my brother so content has made me realize how much a woman...a wife...could add to my life. And I've always wanted children."

She sat up straighter, taken aback by his admission. "Really? I've always thought of you as a confirmed bachelor, content with the way things were." She thought they were alike in that.

With a shrug, he replied, "People change and so do their needs."

"Are you dating anyone seriously, John? Because, well...you haven't shared that with me. And you know we promised that we'd share everything."

He tweaked her nose. "It isn't nice for men to kiss and tell, Ally. How would you feel if we were dating and I shared all the intimate details of our passionate encounters with, say, my brothers, for instance?"

Her cheeks warmed at the mention of intimacy and passion, and she swallowed. "So you are seeing someone?"

"I didn't say that."

Crossing her arms over her chest, she heaved a

sigh of frustration, clearly annoyed by his lack of candor. "Now you're just being obtuse, John David."

"Really?" He flashed her a sexy grin. "I prefer to think of it as enigmatic."

Chapter Eleven

The highway sign read Leadville, 30 Miles, and Maddy squirmed restlessly in her seat, eager to reach their destination.

She and Pete were on their way to visit Mary Beth and Lyle, and she was both excited and nervous. Excited at the prospect of seeing her family again—she missed Mary Beth something terrible—and nervous because she wanted her sister and brother-in-law to adore Pete as much as she did. Mary Beth's approval had always been important to her.

"I can't believe we're actually on our way to see Mary Beth and Lyle."

"Well, the way your sister threatened me with bodily injury over the phone, if I didn't drop everything and bring you at once, made me think it might be a good idea, especially since her husband's a cop." Pete flashed his wife a teasing smile. "Besides, it gives us a chance to take this baby out and see what she can do."

"I assume you're talking about the tank?" Which is how she now referred to her new SUV.

Pete grinned, patting the leather-encased steering wheel with no small amount of affection. "*Shh!* You'll hurt Candy's feelings."

"You named the car Candy?" She rolled her eyes in disbelief. "I thought it was endearing that you had names for your animals, but an SUV? That's weird, in my opinion."

"It's no worse than you calling my private parts 'rocket man.'"

She bit back a smile, recalling the ear-splitting rendition of the Elton John song she'd sung to Pete this morning during their lovemaking. "Well, it is like a heat-seeking missile at times, you've got to admit that."

"Any more comments like that, Mrs. Taggart, and you'll find yourself in the back of this car, flat on your back, and singing the 'Hallelujah Chorus'!"

"Promises, promises," she replied with a naughty smile that went straight to Pete's lap.

Outside the temperature hovered about the freezing mark, but it was getting a whole lot warmer in the car, and Pete thought it best to get his mind on something other than what they'd already done three times that morning. "So tell me about your sister. Is she as pretty as you?" He swerved suddenly to avoid hitting a downed tree limb that had fallen onto the highway and cursed beneath his breath.

"I think she's much prettier. Miles of long red hair, emerald green eyes, and skin like peaches and cream. Mary Beth was quite popular in high school, but she only ever had eyes for Lyle Randolph.''

"That's kind of how it was for me and Bethany. We were high school sweethearts, too. After we graduated, we got engaged, then married two years later. We were really too young, I think, looking back on it now. Of course, hindsight is always twenty-twenty.''

Pete's discussion of his late wife surprised Maddy. He rarely spoke of Bethany, unless he was asked a direct question. And even then he hemmed and hawed before answering, as if fearing it might upset Maddy to hear about her. But quite the opposite was true. She wanted to know everything about Pete's life—his childhood, family, late wife—so she could better understand the man he was today.

"You and Bethany were married quite a long time, so you must have been well suited for each other.''

"Had we been more mature, more worldly, it's likely we wouldn't have ended up with each other in the first place. I think at first we confused lust with love. We came to love each other over the years, but it wasn't that all-consuming, I'll-die-if-I-can't-have-you kind of love.''

Maddy's eyes widened at the admission, but she remained silent, allowing him to continue.

"I think more than anything we were comfortable with each other. And our families seemed to think it was a good match, so we just went along with the flow. I can see now that was a mistake.''

"But you loved her! You said when she died you

were decimated.'' The thought of Pete being that much in love with someone else stabbed into her heart. Being jealous of a dead woman wasn't something Maddy was proud of, but she just couldn't help herself.

"I was. I won't deny it. We'd known each other since we were kids. But I felt anger at Bethany, too. She was so headstrong and sure of herself, knew just what she wanted. She never really liked being a rancher's wife, living on the ranch. She always aspired to more. And she wasn't all that thrilled when she found out she was pregnant. I think it messed up her plans.''

"Her plans?''

Swallowing with some difficulty, he was unable to hide the pain dulling his eyes. ''Yeah. I think Bethany was fixing to leave me, then when she found out she was pregnant, she stayed. But I always had the feeling she felt trapped, not overjoyed by the prospect of motherhood.''

Drawing on whatever tact she possessed, Maddy chose her words carefully. ''It's hard for men to understand that women have goals and aspirations, too, Pete. I'm sure Bethany loved being married to you, wanted your child, but she needed her independence. No woman wants to be just an extension of her husband.''

"You're talking about yourself now, aren't you?''

"I suppose I am. I worked hard, made sacrifices, to get my education and build a career. I don't see a problem with combining both a job and marriage.

Marriage is supposed to be a partnership, not a dictatorship.'' As it had been with her parents. Her father had always had the last word when it came to the three women in the Potter household.

''My mother was content to stay at home and raise us boys,'' Pete said. ''She never complained or said she was unhappy. I like to think Kate Taggart's life was fulfilling. My father adored her, took care of her. I never heard them utter a cross word.''

Maddy didn't think it appropriate to point out that Pete's mom and dad sounded just like Ward and June Cleaver from the fifties TV sitcom *Leave It To Beaver.* ''Would it have done any good for your mother to complain, Pete? Your dad had already carved out her role. What other options did she have? And besides, things were different back then. Women didn't have the opportunities they do now. The sexual revolution was just getting started.''

Pete was getting a bit hot under the collar and adjusted the car's thermostat, lowering the heat. ''Being a wife and mother is a full-time job, Maddy.'' He cracked his window and welcomed in the cold air, then asked,

''Does your sister work?''

She was taken off guard by the question. ''Well, no. Mary Beth's content to stay at home. She's never aspired to anything but being a wife and mother. But that was her decision. No one, including Lyle, made it for her.''

''I like your sister already. She sounds pretty smart to me.''

Maddy stiffened, crossing her arms over her chest, her lips thinning slightly. "And I'm not?"

"Didn't say that. But your sister sounds like a woman who puts her husband first and everything else second. I bet Lyle's a happy man."

"And you're not?"

He gazed over and could tell she was angry at him. Her lips were pinched tight, and her eyes had narrowed. If looks could kill, he'd already be dead. Well, honesty wasn't always the best policy, Pete conceded, but it was the only one he subscribed to. "I didn't say that, Maddy, so quit trying to put words in my mouth."

"You'd better not say anything else, Pete Taggart, or you won't have a wife to complain about."

The turnoff for Leadville appeared just then, and both Maddy and Pete fell silent as he exited the freeway.

"I CAN'T BELIEVE you're really here!" Mary Beth threw her arms about her sister, hugging her fiercely. "Look at you. You're as fat as one of dad's sows."

Maddy laughed despite the insult. "Gee, thanks a lot." Her sister was dressed in a pink-and-green-checked maternity dress that she'd no doubt sewn herself. But Mary Beth didn't look fat; she looked adorable and so very, very happy to be pregnant. "You, too. Isn't it wonderful that we're both as big as barns?"

Pete arched a brow and exchanged a look with Lyle Randolph that said he feared both women were slightly off their rockers. The man apparently agreed, because he held out his hand and said with a shake of his head, "How about a beer? I can use one, if you know what I mean."

With luggage in tow, the foursome entered the comfortable one-level ranch house. It wasn't as large a house as the Taggarts', but it was clean and comfortable, and Mary Beth made it appear cozy with her patchwork quilts and rabbit collection. Rabbits in every size, shape and material appeared everywhere around their home.

"You've done so much with the house since I was here last," Maddy said, trying to take in everything at once, noting the new lace curtains at the living room windows. "I just love it." She was itching to redecorate some of the rooms at Pete's...her...house, but she hadn't mentioned anything to her husband as yet. The nursery would be their first project, then she'd slowly ease into the others.

Because she'd been cursed with a typical redhead's complexion, everything Mary Beth thought or felt was reflected on her face, which was now red with embarrassment. She didn't take compliments too well. "Thanks! And I bet your home is lovely, too. I can't wait to see it, Mad, after hearing you gush over it."

"Why don't you come to visit over Valentine's Day weekend? Sweetheart's holding their annual library fund-raiser, and Pete and I are working on the committee."

"They're going to play old fogy songs," Pete warned his new sister-in-law. "So be prepared."

"Hey, us old fogies will like that, right, Mares?" Lyle asked with a grin, slipping his arm about his wife's expanded middle and kissing her cheek, making it obvious to everyone in the room that the high school sweethearts remained very much in love.

Still irked from their earlier conversation, Maddy made a face at her husband, which didn't go unnoticed by Mary Beth and Lyle. "Don't pay any attention to Pete. He's just being obtuse."

"Ah, Pete," Lyle said, hoping to ease the irritation he noted on the newlyweds' faces, "Maddy tells us you're ranching over in Sweetheart. How many head are you running?"

"Lyle always wanted to be a rancher," Mary Beth interjected, "but he felt it was his duty to follow his dad into law enforcement. But he's still crazy about horses and cows. I think he would have made an adorable cowboy, don't you?"

Pete grinned at the tall man's mortified expression—Lyle Randolph was actually blushing! "I've got about two hundred head on four hundred acres, and you're welcome to come play rancher anytime you want, Lyle." He liked Maddy's brother-in-law, so it was easy for him to make the gesture. "I've got plenty of chores to go around, and I'd welcome the help."

"Thanks, I might just do that. Who's taking care of things while you're gone?"

"Hired a couple of boys who live down the road

from me to tend the stock and feed the dog while we're away."

"And you're not worried?"

"Hell, yes, I'm worried. Though they're good boys, they're still kids. But I thought it was important that Maddy see her sister." He glanced at his wife and winked, and was finally rewarded with a hundred-watt smile that made him feel all was right with the world again.

After lunch, Maddy followed Lyle into his den to look at the oil painting he was working on—a new hobby he had just taken up to reduce stress—while Pete followed Maddy's sister into the kitchen to help her clean up.

"I couldn't help notice that my sister seems very happy, Pete, if not a little distracted. Are you two having problems?"

With a shrug, he took the dish she handed him and began wiping it. "Just the usual newlywed stuff, I guess. You know, getting adjusted to each other and all that."

"I'm glad to hear it's nothing more than that."

"We don't agree on women working after they're married, and Maddy refuses to believe that I'm in love with her, but other than that everything's just hunky-dory."

Mary Beth smiled softly at the dejected look on his face, wiped her hands on a paper towel and offered him a chair at the kitchen table, taking a seat next to him. "Because of that quilt legend she told me about?"

He nodded, trying to hide his disgust. "I've tried to show Maddy in countless ways how crazy I am about her, but she's convinced that I'm only behaving this way because the stupid legend foretold of our marriage and falling in love."

"It's really rather romantic, I think. But I can see how it would be frustrating for you. Maddy can be awfully stubborn at times."

"I'll say."

"You mustn't be too hard on her, Pete. A lot of the reason Maddy acts and feels the way she does has to do with her relationship with our father. They never got along well, and she never really believed he loved her. Though he does, I can assure you.

"Dad asks about her all the time, would love to see her, but she continues to refuse. Maddy's convinced herself that he's responsible for my mother's death, and she's never forgiven him for being so devoted to his pigs.

"She felt slighted when we were growing up. She wanted to be the apple of his eye, the most important thing in the world to him, and she wasn't. It was hard for Maddy to play second fiddle to a smelly swine."

"I'm sure Mr. Potter and I would hit it off then. I'm pretty passionate about my animals. Of course, I'm pretty damn passionate about Maddy, and she knows it."

"I think Maddy has a difficult time believing that any man could really love her because of the way she thinks our father felt toward her."

Pete had sensed that first day they'd met that Maddy had issues about her father, and he was sorry to hear he'd been right, especially since hearing Mary Beth's assertion that Maddy felt unlovable. Damn fool woman!

"If your dad loves Maddy, cares about her, why doesn't he try to patch things up? That doesn't make any sense."

"Andrew Potter's a proud man, and every bit as stubborn as Maddy. I guess that's where she gets it from. And over the years he did make a few gestures—Christmas and birthday cards, messages left on her answering machine—but they were never acknowledged, and after a while he gave up."

"Maddy's so open and loving. It's hard to believe she'd do something like that."

"Maddy was like a hurt animal, and she wanted to hurt back. And she did, with her indifference. I guess my sister thought she was giving dad a taste of his own medicine. And in a sense, she has."

"I take it you and your father are still in touch?"

"Yes," Mary Beth replied, toying with the gingham tablecloth. "We see each other from time to time, and he's made it clear that he wants to be part of my child's life. I think he knows the shortcomings he had as a father and wants to make up for them in some way."

"And you're going to let him?"

"Definitely. I think children need grandparents, don't you?"

"I do. I only wish my parents were still alive to

take on the role. I guess Maddy's dad will be the only grandfather our baby has.''

Noting the way he said ''our,'' Mary Beth felt relieved and happy for her sister. There was no doubt in her mind that Pete Taggart wanted to raise the baby as his own. Her sister was a very lucky woman. There weren't too many Sir Galahads left in the world. But then, she suspected that Maddy had already found that out after her experience with David Lassiter.

Reaching out, she covered Pete's hand. ''Which is why we need to help Maddy and my father swallow their pride and reconcile,'' she said finally. ''Andrew's not getting any younger—he'll be sixty in March—and I think if he and Maddy could work out their differences, they'd both be the better for it. I know deep in her heart Maddy still loves Dad and needs him in her life.'' And she knew her father was eager to make amends. It was all he'd spoken about the last time he'd called.

''She won't like the interference. Maddy thinks I'm too bossy and opinionated as it is.''

''I know. She told me.'' The redhead eased into a smile and tried to explain. ''Maddy's used to being independent, Pete. She left home right after high school and was on her own, for the most part. I tried to help her when I could. But I was newly married to Lyle, and there just wasn't much I could do. We didn't have any money to spare, and she wouldn't have accepted it at any rate.''

"Maddy wants to run her own business, and I'm not keen on the idea."

"Didn't you fall in love with the woman you found stranded in her automobile? She hasn't changed, and she's not likely to. Maddy's worked hard for what she has, and I doubt she'll agree to give it up. Not without a fight."

"But I want to protect her, take care of her and the baby."

Heaving a sigh, the pregnant woman rose from her chair. She liked Pete Taggart, thought he and her sister were a good match, but the road ahead of them was not going to be easy, not with the different ideologies they possessed.

"Looks like Maddy met her match when she married you, Pete. You're as stubborn as my sister, and that doesn't bode well for your future happiness. I hope you two can come to some sort of understanding."

Her eyes filled with worry, and he squeezed her hand reassuringly. "Don't worry, Mary Beth. We'll work things out. You'll see. Maddy will come around to my way of thinking. I'm sure of it."

But Mary Beth wasn't sure, and she worried for her new brother-in-law and the sister she loved.

SEATED ON THE SOFA in Lyle's den, her feet up on the old restored trunk that served as a coffee table, Maddy studied the man who was her brother-in-law.

Lyle Randolph was a big man, tall in stature, with wide shoulders and a big, beefy neck. He appeared intimidating to those who worked under him, or to those criminals unlucky enough to cross his path. But deep down he was a kind soul with a big heart.

Lyle was the big brother Maddy never had, and a surrogate father when the occasion called for it. He was a good listener who said what he thought and doled out sound advice when asked; Maddy desperately needed his advice now.

"How do you feel about women in the workplace, Lyle?"

He took a swig of his beer, contemplated the question for a few moments, then said, "I've resented some of the women I've been forced to hire over the years. They weren't always the best candidates for the job, but we had to hire them or risk losing state funding. Affirmative action and all that bureaucratic nonsense."

Job discrimination in the workplace had always been a touchy subject, and that wasn't likely to change anytime soon. Affirmative action had left a bad taste in a lot of people's mouths, but women needed the laws that the government and state localities had set down in order to prove their worth in a male-dominated workplace. They may have never been given the chance otherwise.

"Are you glad Mary Beth never worked outside the home?"

He plopped down on the sofa next to her, the cushions sinking deep beneath his weight. "I guess I am, like any good male chauvinist pig." He winked at her.

"You're the last male I'd pin that label on, Lyle. You've always supported and encouraged Mary Beth in all of her decisions."

"That's true. And I wouldn't have objected had she wanted to work, but I'm happy as hell she didn't. I like having her home, cooking my meals, waiting up for me when I get home late. I know it sounds selfish and archaic to someone as liberated as you, Maddy, but that's the way I feel."

His confession wasn't quite what she'd been hoping for. Lyle's sentiments sounded too similar to her husband's. "Pete wants me to quit working and stay home after the baby's born."

His eyes lit with sudden understanding. His sister-in-law was usually so self-assured about everything, but now Maddy seemed confused and conflicted. "And how do you feel about that, as if I didn't already know?"

She pushed playfully on his arm. "I don't want to give up my work, Lyle. I love it. And I'm good at it. I don't mind cutting back, working part-time till the baby's born. But after that I don't see why I couldn't just bring the child into the workplace with me. I'm going to be my own boss. I won't have to answer to anyone but myself."

The defiance she wore like a suit of armor didn't bode well. "Except your husband, I take it?"

Her sigh spoke volumes. "Pete's rather old-fashioned. He doesn't believe a woman should work outside the home. His mother never did, so he doesn't see the need for me to."

"Have you spoken to him about your feelings, tried to make him understand?"

"Of course, but he's stubborn and opinionated and—"

"You love him."

She nodded, and her eyes filled with tears. "I don't want this issue to come between us, but I'm worried it already has. We had a fight in the car on the way over here."

"Nobody ever said marriage was an easy row to hoe, Mad. You're going to disagree from time to time, that's only to be expected, and you'll have to figure out the best way to work it out."

"Why can't Pete be as levelheaded and sensible as you?"

Leadville's chief of police threw back his head and laughed till his sides ached. "Mary Beth would just love to comment on the exalted picture you've drawn of me. I'm positive she would have a lot to say on the subject."

He pointed toward the easel. "Maybe you should be painting the pictures, instead of me."

"Maybe you should take a compliment when it's given, you ungracious oaf."

"Ah, that's more like the girl I know and love." He wrapped his arms about her, and they felt welcoming and so familiar. "You're a smart girl, Maddy. When the time's right, you'll know just what to do."

"Pardon the pun, but that sounds like a *cop-out* to me. And what if I don't? What if I make a big mess of everything?'' It wouldn't be the first time, but now she had too much to lose—her heart, her husband, her entire world.

"Only you can decide what's most important to you, Maddy,'' Lyle told her.

"Yeah? Well, in case nobody's told you, decisions haven't been my strong suit of late.''

Chapter Twelve

"You were so clever, Maddy, to come up with the idea of issuing the invitations to the library fund-raiser in the form of Valentines to everyone in town," Ella said, beaming. "I can't tell you how many nice comments I've had, and how many responses from folks who say they are coming. This is going to be our largest event yet, just you wait and see."

Maddy looked about the high school gymnasium with a healthy dose of skepticism. The bleachers were old, the basketball hoops still in place, and she doubted anything short of a miracle could turn the place into a cozy, romantic setting for the dance in the space of two short weeks. They might have to rename the event Let Me Call You Sweatsocks, due the persistent, unpleasant odor that hung in the air.

"Thanks, Ella. But are you sure this gymnasium is the best location for the event? I realize it's large and can accommodate a lot of people, but it definitely lacks atmosphere."

"Not to worry, dear. My decorating committee has assured me that everything will look splendid."

Maddy stared at the older woman as if she had lost her mind. "But *I'm* head of that committee!" she said, pointing to herself.

"Yes, I know. Which is why I have no doubt that you and that sweet husband of yours, along with Allison and John, will perform miracles. I'd get started sooner rather than later, though. Time waits for no man, as they say. And we have the school's permission to begin decorating the gymnasium in the evenings, starting tomorrow night."

Maddy tried to sound enthusiastic, knowing how excited Ella was, and not wanting to burst her bubble. But she wasn't convinced, not by a long shot, that she'd be able to pull this off. "I'll get right on it."

The older woman's smile suddenly melted into one of concern. "You're not overdoing, are you, Maddy? I couldn't help but notice that you're now in the family way. And by the size of you, I'd say you were going to deliver twins."

Maddy felt her cheeks warm at the woman's bluntness. She would never get used to Ella Grady's lack of tact. "I'm feeling fine. And, well, women in my family tend to have large babies." She had no idea if that was true. In fact, she rather doubted it since she and Mary Beth had both weighed under eight pounds when they were born.

"Gracious! Your delivery's not going to be a piece of cake then, is it? Suzanne Walters's last child weighed in at ten pounds, fourteen ounces, and she was in labor for over twenty-three hours. Poor dear. I hear the anesthetic had worn off totally by the time she delivered, and she behaved like a raving maniac, screaming at all the nurses, and telling poor Brad that she hated him. Her husband was just beside himself.''

Maddy swallowed. Though she wasn't exactly afraid of having this baby, she didn't want to hear horror stories, either. They tended to make her dwell on the negative, and that wasn't wise for a first-timer like herself.

''I'm sure everything will be just fine, Ella.'' Pete was certain to make sure of that. The exasperating man was a regular mother hen, continuing to lecture her on what foods she should and shouldn't eat, how much exercise she should get, and a host of other things. The only thing he hadn't taken her to task over was the amount of lovemaking they indulged in, sharing her opinion that sex, and lots of it was just what the doctor ordered.

''When's the baby due?'' Ella wanted to know. ''I'd like to give you a shower to thank you for all the hard work you've done for the library.''

''That's very kind of you.'' Maddy was touched by the offer, but also concerned. The question she'd been dreading had just been posed, and she saw no alternative but to stretch the truth a bit, telling herself that it really wasn't lying. ''Dr. Peterson couldn't be exact, but she's predicting sometime in the fall. Of course, with first babies it could come earlier or later. It's so hard to predict.''

The explanation seemed to satisfy the woman, filling Maddy with relief. "Well, I've got a million and one things left to do," the librarian said, bussing her on the cheek, "so I'll leave you to work your magic. See you soon, Maddy dear.''

As soon as Ella had shut the door behind her, Maddy heaved a deep sigh at the impossibility of the task ahead of her. Turning a sow's ear into a silk purse wouldn't be easy.

Magic had come into her life when she least expected it, or wanted it, through the quilt legend. And now when she really needed a large dose to pull this dance off, there was none to be found. "Figures," she said, taking out her notebook.

TWO DAYS LATER, Allison looked up from the pile of red construction paper in front of her and made a face of disgust. "I never thought I'd say this, but I never want to see another red paper heart as long as I live. We've cut out hundreds of these already, and I'm sick to death of them.''

"Yeah, well you don't have to paste the white doily edges on them," John complained, holding one up for everyone's inspection. The lace trim was lopsided and the white glue visible, giving testimony to the fact that John was a finer vet than he was an artist. "I've got better things to do with my time than play with paper and paste.''

"Me, too," Pete agreed. "We were out of our

minds to agree to help Ella with this project. Of course, *we* didn't agree, did we? *You* did," he said, pointing an accusing finger at his wife.

Hearing the frustration in their voices, Maddy empathized completely. She, too, was sick of making Valentine decorations. But she knew someone had to do it, and they had volunteered. Sort of.

She set a plate of cookies down on the dining room table, where they were all working. "Maybe these will cheer you up. They're chocolate chip."

"You got a bourbon chaser to go along with them?" Pete asked, reaching for one and nearly spilling the plastic glue bottle in the process. "Dang it all."

"Your hearts look like the hind end of a mule, Pete Taggart," Allison remarked. "Who taught you how to draw anyway?"

His grin was downright nasty. "I can quit anytime. And you're not exactly Michelangelo, you know." He held up the red heart he'd just fashioned. "Besides, I tend to think of these as breasts. They look kinda like them, don't you think?"

"Leave it to you to think of that, bro."

"None of you are allowed to quit," Maddy informed her committee. "Especially you, Pete, since you'll be hanging the disco ball I've rented."

"Disco ball!" He looked horrified at the prospect. "I hate disco music! Where'd you find that anyway? And why? I thought you had your heart set on old fogy songs."

Maddy flashed her husband a long-suffering look

and, without comment, turned her attention to Allison. "How are you and Mark coming along with the refreshments? Are we going to have enough?"

Concern marred the woman's features. "I thought so, but then Ella called this morning to inform me that we've just received another fifty acceptances. Guess we'll have to make more cupcakes and cookies, and those miniature cream puffs Mark's so good at."

"Well, if there's anything I can do, let me know. I'm quite willing to bake, or—"

"You will not!" Pete said adamantly. "You're doing way too much as it is. You need to slow down, Maddy, delegate more responsibility. There are others in this town who could help out with the fundraiser. You don't have to do everything yourself."

Crossing her arms over her chest, she counted silently to ten, trying to keep her temper in check by reminding herself that her autocratic husband had only her best interests at heart. "Really? And who might they be?" She'd already asked everyone in town she could think of. And though they all thought it a very worthwhile cause, and that she was wonderful for taking on the responsibility, every last one of them had made an excuse.

"When I started getting excuses like, 'my toilet's been backing up every day and I can't possibly leave it,' I figured I was on my own."

Pete thought a moment. "How about Ed Bixby? He owes us for that car purchase."

"He owes *you*. And I've already asked Ed to help. He's lending us an old '57 Chevy convertible that we're going to use as a decoration—a prop, I guess you could call it.''

John's eyes lit. "Cool! When's it coming?"

"Not until the night before the dance. And you and Pete are not authorized to go anywhere near it."

"Damn! I've always wanted to neck in the back seat of a '57 Chevy," John said, eyes twinkling.

"Who are you planning to make out with, John?" Allison asked with the lift of an eyebrow, doing her best to appear nonchalant. "Do enlighten us, Dr. Taggart."

"A gentleman never kisses and tells. But if you're interested in participating, I can—"

"I never said any such thing, John Taggart!" The blonde's cheeks turned as bright as the red heart clutched in her hand.

Maddy and Pete exchanged amused glances; John laughed out loud.

Allison merely fumed, then said, "I don't know what's come over you lately, John. You've been saying strange things and acting quite odd."

The vet tilted back his chair, picked up a handful of the decorated hearts lying in front of him and tossed them in the air. One landed on top of Allison's head. "Why, it must be love. All these hearts and romantic notions have gotten hold of me." He winked, and her mouth dropped open. "Who would have ever thought?"

SATURDAY'S MAIL BROUGHT two unexpected missives. One was a letter from Mary Beth and Lyle apologizing for not being able to attend the fundraiser. They'd enclosed a check for twenty-five dollars as a donation.

"Oh, shoot," Maddy said, disappointment edging her words. "My sister won't be coming to the dance after all."

Pete rested his chin on her shoulder and tried to read the letter. "How come? I thought it was all set."

"Apparently half of Lyle's police department has come down with the flu. He's shorthanded and has to work."

"Too bad. I was looking forward to his visit, to showing him the ropes." He'd sensed upon meeting Lyle Randolph that they were destined to become good friends. They had a lot in common, not the least of which was their taste in women.

She continued reading, then finally smiled. "They're going to come in a few weeks, as soon as Lyle can get everything straightened out at work."

"Who's the other card from?" Pete asked. The envelope was pink and just the right size for a valentine. "Do you have a secret admirer you're not telling me about?" He reached around, cradled her stomach and kissed her on the cheek. "I'm a jealous man, sweetheart."

Pete's touch always elicited the predictable response, and Maddy's heart fluttered madly. "You're insatiable! We just got out of bed a couple of hours ago, and you're already thinking about—" She shook her head, opening the envelope that had no return address, though the postmark registered Iowa.

Her heart went from fluttering to pounding, but this time it was nerves that had caused the reaction. "Maybe I'll open this up later."

Turning her about to face him, he said, "Not a chance. If you've got an admirer, I want to know who it is, so I can beat the crap outta him."

When he saw the trepidation on her face, his teasing smile faded and he asked, "Is it from Lassiter? Has that creep sent you a Valentine?" He'd kill the bastard if he tried to come between them. No one, not Lassiter, not God himself, was going to take Maddy and the baby away from him this time.

"No!" she said, shaking her head and handing the card to him. "Here, you read it."

Tearing open the envelope, Pete read the valentine's flowery sentiment, then glanced down at the signature and relief washed over him. "It's from your dad." He tried to hand it back, but she refused to take it.

"I'm not interested. Just toss it in the trash."

"Maddy—" his voice was full of censure "—you don't mean that." He followed her into the kitchen, where she began busying herself with cleaning out the refrigerator.

"Heavens, how old is this milk?" she asked no one in particular, removing the carton and sniffing the contents, then pouring it all down the sink.

Since Pete had bought the milk just two days before, he figured his wife was pretty upset. "Don't try and hide from this, Maddy. Your sister told me a bit about what's been going on between you and your dad, and that he's tried to contact you from time to time.''

''Mary Beth had no right to tell you.''

''Your sister had every right. I'm your husband. And the least you can do is meet the man halfway.''

''What's between me and my father is none of your business, Pete. It has nothing to do with us.''

He placed his palm on her abdomen. ''And what about the baby? Andrew Potter is this child's grandfather. And I'm a firm believer in children having grandparents.''

''Too bad. My baby doesn't need a grandfather like that.''

''*Our* baby, don't you mean? And he does need him, Maddy, just the same as you do. The man's getting older. I think he realizes the mistakes he's made and wants to make amends. Why can't you let him?''

Tears filled her eyes. ''I don't expect you to understand, Pete. You came from a loving, nurturing family. Your dad was always there for you. Well, mine wasn't. He was preoccupied with his pigs. And when he wasn't, he went around the house issuing orders to everyone, including my mother. It's his fault she died so young.''

''Now, Maddy, be fair. You told me your mom died because her heart was bad. How can you blame your dad for that?''

''Because he was never there for her. She ran the

house, took care of me and my sister, and he gave her no help whatsoever. Is it any wonder her poor heart gave out?''

Her wounded look ripped at his gut, and he wrapped his arms about her, hoping to ease the pain. ''Your mother obviously loved your father. She stayed with him for a very long time.''

The fears she felt poured out of Maddy. ''My mother was trapped. She had nowhere else to go. She had no education, no money, no—''

''Did she tell you that? Is that why you're so eager to retain your independence?''

She shook her head. ''My mother was like yours, never complaining, always doing what my father asked of her. But unlike your mother, my dad didn't dote on her. He hardly knew she existed, that any of us existed. He was too busy attending fairs, winning blue ribbons, discussing the bloodlines of his pigs with other farmers just like him.''

''I've done all those things you've mentioned, and will continue to do them, Maddy. It's part of ranching. So how does that make me different from your dad?'' Pete asked.

''You just are. Yes, you're overbearing at times—'' Maddy noted his brows raised at that ''—but you're also thoughtful, kind and considerate. You make me feel special, important—something he never did.''

''You are special, Maddy, and I love you.''

Her eyes softened. ''I'm beginning to believe that.''

"Believe it. But I also think you're making a big mistake by not making amends with your dad. He's getting older, and I know he wants to see you. Your sister told me as much."

She covered her face, trying to block out the image of her father the last time she saw him, standing on the front porch of their home, waving goodbye and not really understanding why she had chosen to leave. "I can't." She shook her head. "There's too much unhappiness between us."

"You're a strong woman, Maddy Taggart, just like generations of Taggart women before you. And you have a big heart. Try to find room in it for an old man who's willing to admit that he made a mistake. At least, think about it. Will you do that much?"

She wiped the tears from her face with the back of her hand and nodded. "All right." But only for Pete's sake would she think about it. Because he'd asked her to, and because she loved him.

And because maybe, just maybe, he loved her, too.

"PETE, FOR HEAVEN'S SAKE, be careful! You're going to break your neck if you're not." Terrified that he was going to fall, Maddy shielded her eyes as she looked up at her husband perched precariously on top of a thirty-foot extension ladder as he attempted to hang the disco ball from the ceiling rafter.

Her committee—all four of them—had met at the gymnasium after dinner to make the final preparations for the Valentine's Day fund-raiser, which would be held tomorrow evening. Come hell or high water, which wasn't far from the truth. It had been raining like crazy all day. The rain continued to pelt the aging aluminum roof like a spray of bullets.

"*Shh,* Maddy!" John cautioned, keeping pressure on the bottom rung of the ladder so it wouldn't slip. "You'll make him nervous, and he'll lose his concentration."

"Dammit! I need my socket wrench," Pete shouted down, sounding totally frustrated. "I think I left it at home on the kitchen counter."

"I'll run and get it," John offered.

Both Maddy and Allison stared horrified as he started to back away from the ladder. They shouted in unison, "No!"

"I'll drive home and get it," Maddy said. "I know just where he left it, and it won't take me but a few minutes."

"Pete won't like that," Allison warned her friend, grateful Maddy's husband was too high up to hear what they were saying.

"Well, it's time my husband learned that I'm perfectly capable of doing things for myself."

Allison held her hands up in front of her. "Hey, you won't get any objection from me. I'm just telling you that your shadow will not approve of your driving out in the rain."

"Ally's right, Maddy," John said over his shoulder, then glanced up at his brother again, who was still fiddling with the wiring. "It'd be better if I went."

"And leave Pete stranded up there on the ladder?" She shook her head. "I don't think so. Now just continue on with what you're doing, Ally. The crepe paper still needs to be draped and all those lovely hearts you've made hung. I won't be gone long."

A moment later, Pete, having noted that his wife had donned her parka and was heading for the exit door, shouted down from his perch, "Maddy, where in the hell do you think you're going? Come back here!"

But Maddy merely waved and smiled, pretending she didn't hear a word he'd said. "Be right back."

BUT SHE WASN'T. Forty-five minutes had elapsed since her departure and Maddy still hadn't returned.

Pete paced the wooden floor, plowing agitated fingers through his hair, and looking like a madman in the throes of torture. "I'm going after her. Something's happened. I can feel it in my gut."

Not again, God! Please, not again.

"Don't be such an alarmist, Pete! I'm sure Maddy's perfectly fine. She probably had trouble finding the tool you wanted, that's all." But Allison was also beginning to worry. She'd tried reaching Maddy on her cell phone during a bathroom break, unbeknownst to Pete or John, and there hadn't been any answer. Of course, Maddy was notorious for shutting off her phone, so that could explain her lack of response. At least, Ally prayed that was the reason.

John squeezed his brother's shoulder. "Ally's

right, Pete. Let's give Maddy a few more minutes.'' He glanced at his watch, his frown deepening. ''If she's not back by eight, I'll take the truck and go look for her.''

''I'll go,'' Pete insisted. ''She's my wife.''

''And you'll make her feel that you're spying on her, that she's incapable of doing anything on her own,'' the young woman pointed out.

Just then the heavy door opened, and Maddy came sailing in, drenched to the bone but looking none the worse for wear.

''Where the hell have you been?'' Pete's voice thundered off the walls.

''Sorry it took so long. My sister called just when I was about to leave to come back, and I got caught in a long conversation about her doctor's appointment.''

''We were starting to worry, Maddy,'' Allison said, hoping to buffer Pete's rage. The man looked ready to spit nails or faint, she couldn't decide which. ''Next time phone and let us know you're all right, okay?''

''Why wouldn't I be? It's just a little rain.'' Removing her jacket, she shook it out, spraying water everywhere.

Sucking in his anger, Pete stepped forward. ''Rain that could just as easily have turned to sleet this time of year,'' he pointed out, dragging her into his arms and crushing her to his chest. ''You had me scared half to death, woman.''

Noting the fear in his eyes, the anguish in his

voice, and feeling his rapid heartbeat against her ear, Maddy felt somewhat guilty for making Pete worry so. But she was determined that he treat her like a responsible adult, not a child. "I'm sorry you were worried. But as you can see, I'm perfectly fine, and you were concerned for nothing."

"But, Maddy—"

Reaching into her purse, she pulled out the tool and handed it to him, determined not to let him have the last word. "Here's the wrench thing you wanted. I hope it's the right one."

"It is."

"Good. Then let's get back to work. We've got a lot to do before tomorrow night."

"And we thought Ella Grady was a slave driver," Allison told John, dragging him out of earshot.

"I think Maddy's corporate tendencies are coming to the forefront," he said. "It's not hard to envision her directing an office full of people, is it?"

"Your brother seems to think she's incompetent and totally helpless. Maybe you should have a talk with him."

"Me?" John's eyes widened, and he looked dismayed. "Why me? I'm the younger brother, remember? Pete doesn't like being lectured to, and he especially won't like it coming from me." The last time Mark had tried to counsel him after Bethany's death, Pete had punched him in the face, blackening his eye. John wasn't eager for a repeat performance.

Clasping his arm, Allison steered him toward the yellow Chevy that would soon be decorated with life-size cardboard cutouts of Richard Gere and Julia Roberts that the movie house in Colorado Springs had loaned them. "They love each other, John. A love like theirs is hard to find these days. We've got to do everything in our power to see that they remain together."

Eyes softening, he slid his fingertip down her cheek. "I never knew you to be such a romantic, Ally. This is a whole new side of you I'm seeing."

"I adore Maddy. And I know how stubborn your brother can be. Remember what happened to his last marriage? Things were not going well between Pete and Bethany before she died. Bethany had entertained thoughts of leaving him, though I don't think she would have."

John's face registered shock. "What? I had no idea."

"I kept it from you, fearing you'd tell Pete and hurt him even more than he'd already been hurt." She crossed her arms over her chest.

"Now, are you going to talk to your brother or not?"

He glanced behind them, caressing the soft leather of the rolled-and-tucked seats. "Will you sit with me in the back seat if I do?"

She eyed both John and the car skeptically, wondering if he was going through some kind of early male menopause. "All right. But there's to be no necking. Is that understood?"

"How about if I just cop a—"

"John Taggart! Act your age, for heaven's sake! You're a respected veterinarian."

"True. Which means I know all about animal instinct."

A strange flush came over Allison for which she had no explanation. "I've changed my mind. I won't sit with you."

"Chicken."

Her chin came up. "Don't flatter yourself."

He reached into the pocket of his coat and withdrew a paper heart, handing it to her. "Will you be my valentine?"

Her heart skipped a beat as she stared at the offering, then noting the smug look on his face, anger took over and she drew herself up to her full five feet eight inches. "Stop this nonsense at once, John David! I will not be your valentine, I will not sit in the back seat of the car with you, and I will not dance with you tomorrow evening, if you don't stop this ridiculous teasing."

He shrugged, looking nonplussed by her outburst. "Okay."

Feeling more confused than ever, Allison watched him walk away. "He's been sniffing too much paste," she said to herself. "His brain cells are dying." That had to be the explanation for his very strange behavior.

Chapter Thirteen

The gymnasium looked magical. Maddy had to admit, as her gaze traveled around the large room, that they'd done an amazing job of transforming the unattractive sports arena into a romantic setting.

Tiny white Christmas lights twinkled overhead against a black canvas backdrop, creating the illusion of stars against a night sky. The disco ball Pete had painstakingly hung turned slowly, the red and white spotlights reflecting off it, and turning the room and dance floor into a dazzling display of light and shadow.

Red hearts hung suspended from every imaginable place, including the basketball standards, and red and white crepe paper had been draped around the poles and light fixtures.

"It looks wonderful, sweetheart," Pete said, kissing her cheek. "Congratulations!"

"It does look nice, doesn't it," she replied, feeling proud of their efforts. The only thing missing was the heart-shaped ice sculpture she had ordered for the buffet table, which had been dropped during delivery. The driver had apologized for "breaking her heart," but Maddy hadn't found the man's comment the least bit amusing.

"I didn't do it by myself. I couldn't have done any of this without you, Allison and John."

"And don't forget Ed Bixby."

She glanced across the dance floor toward the yellow '57 Chevy. "The car does look rather spiffy. And everyone is clamoring to have their photos taken with Richard and Julia, for a price, of course. That idea, Mr. Taggart, was inspired, brilliant even."

"Some of your creativity must be rubbing off."

Allison approached just then in a short red leather skirt and jacket with high heels to match. She looked sexy and svelte, and Maddy felt like a cow standing next to her. "I've never seen so many people turn out for one event before," she said. "The ladies' room is a nightmare."

"Yes, isn't it wonderful?" Ella said, coming up to wrap her arm about Maddy's waist, her round cheeks rosy with pleasure. "We've sold three hundred and fifty-five tickets and raised over fifty-three hundred dollars for the library. Can you imagine? I just can't tell you how thrilled I am." She clapped her hands excitedly.

"All thanks to you, Maddy, and your decorating committee. Allison, that means you, too." Ella gazed up at the rancher. "And Pete, everyone is agog at that ball you stuck up on the ceiling. Why, it's lovely. I've never seen anything like it."

Which didn't surprise Pete. Ella wasn't the disco inferno type, though he noticed she wore low leather pumps this evening instead of her usual tennis shoes. Who was she planning to dance with? he wondered. Did Ella Grady have a beau?

"We were happy to help, Ella," he said finally, and Maddy fought the urge to roll her eyes at him, remembering her husband's long list of complaints and his vow never to volunteer for anything again.

"You're such a dear boy, Peter. And now at long last you're going to be a father and have a son or daughter who will no doubt have the distinctive Taggart blue eyes. You must be so excited."

Maddy had said David Lassiter's eyes were brown, so it was anyone's guess what color the child's eyes would be. Pete didn't care, as long as the baby was healthy and had all of its fingers and toes. Maddy was concerned what people would say if the child didn't resemble either one of them, but Pete figured they'd cross that bridge when the time came. No sense borrowing trouble, as his mother used to say.

"You're looking good tonight, Mrs. Taggart," Allison said with a wink. "Is that one of the dresses we purchased?"

"Yes, and I feel like an overgrown watermelon." Maddy gazed down at her prominent bulge and grimaced. "I don't think the green-and-red plaid combination is too flattering." The dress had looked adorable on the mannequin, but once she'd put it on she realized the plaid only served to make her look larger. And she didn't need any help with that!

"Nonsense, girl! You look lovely." Ella gave Maddy's waist a squeeze. "All pregnant women feel like two-ton heifers. That's just natural. And there are some in this room that aren't pregnant who look a whole lot fatter than you."

Maddy forced a smile at the left-handed compliment. "Thanks, I think."

"Oh, look, there's Sheriff Dobbs," the older woman said, her cheeks flushing slightly. "I must go and thank him for helping out with the parking situation. All those cars. It was a Herculean task." She gave an airy wave and departed.

"So that's the way the wind blows," Pete muttered to himself, noting Frank Dobbs's heightened color as Ella took his hand. The man was obviously smitten with the spinster, and she with him. Well good, Pete thought. He hoped things worked out for the older couple. Now that he'd found his soul mate he wanted everyone to be just as happy and in love.

The smooth, silken strains of Frank Sinatra's voice suddenly blared out from the loudspeakers, and Pete clasped his wife by the hand. "I believe this is our dance, sweetheart."

"It's doubtful we'll be able to get close enough to dance," Maddy said gesturing to her belly. Her husband whispered something in her ear that made her blush.

Watching the couple depart, Allison heaved a sigh. They looked deliriously happy. She hoped things would remain that way.

"Why, Allison Montgomery, don't you look like a fashion plate tonight?"

Allison cringed at the sound of Vivian Helmsley's voice, but pasted on a smile nonetheless. Vivian's husband, Willis, owned the only auto repair business in town. If she wanted her aging Toyota worked on, Allison couldn't afford to alienate the annoying woman, though she certainly felt like it. Vivian had a well-earned reputation as a notorious gossip and troublemaker.

"I guess you've heard that Maddy and Pete Taggart are expecting? It seems kinda sudden, don't you think? I mean—they were only married a short time ago. And she looks quite large for—" she counted on her fingers "—six weeks."

"Maddy and Pete have known each other for a while, Vivian, so I don't see anything at all strange or sudden about it." Ally figured it was better to allude to a previous affair than have the nosy woman figure out the other.

Behind her tortoiseshell rims, Vivian's myopic brown eyes widened. "Oh, you mean—"

Allison shrugged. "It's really none of my business, or yours, either, for that matter, Viv," she reminded the dark-haired woman.

Vivian smoothed the skirt of her blue chiffon dress—the same dress, Allison noted, that she had worn as mother of the groom when her son, Forrest, had gotten married two years before. "I was just making conversation," she stated, not looking the least bit contrite. "Everyone in town's been talking about them. It's not just me who's noticed."

Mark came up then, and Allison could have kissed him. In fact, she did, quite to his surprise, giving Vivian more fodder for her gossip mill.

"Mark! Thank goodness you're here. I was hoping you hadn't forgotten about our dance. You'll excuse us, won't you, Viv?" Without waiting for a reply, she dragged the poor man onto the dance floor, leaving Vivian to stare openmouthed after them.

"I know I'm irresistible, Ally," Mark said, when they were a safe distance away, "but what's going on? Why are you so eager to dance?"

"I can't stand Vivian Helmsley. She's been gossiping about Pete and Maddy, speculating on the due date of their baby."

"Ah, I should have guessed." He clasped her hand and pulled her closer. "You smell good, like vanilla and cinnamon."

"Gee, thanks! I guess those would be two of your favorite scents?"

"Not too romantic a line, huh?"

"I'd practice a bit before trying it out on some unsuspecting female."

"No chance of that. Sweetheart's not exactly bursting with single women. And anyway all the good ones are already taken."

"Well, thanks a lot!"

He grinned at her mock outrage. "You don't count, Ally. You're like my little sister."

"Mark," Ally began, choosing her words carefully, "have you noticed anything strange or unusual about John's behavior lately? Is something bothering him that I don't know about?"

You could say that! Mark thought but didn't. "Not that I've noticed, but then, I've been kinda busy, what with Pete's wedding and now this event. I haven't had much time to sit down and chat with either of my brothers. Why? Have you noticed something?"

Distracted, she stepped on his foot then mumbled an apology. "It's nothing, I guess. Probably just my overworked imagination playing tricks on me."

"If you say so."

She took in the dark cut of his suit, the broadness of his shoulders, and wondered what he was doing at the dance alone. "You look very nice this evening. How come you didn't bring a date?"

"No time. Like I said, I've been busy."

"Too busy to get married again?" Allison persisted. "Don't you want a mother for your kids?"

Used to Allison's abruptness, Mark merely shrugged. "Guess I've still got a bitter taste in my mouth after the last go-around. I'm not eager to get involved again. Too painful. Too time-consuming."

"Well, nobody ever thought Pete would find the woman of his dreams, but he has. I think Maddy's just perfect for him."

"Guess I'll have to go out during the next blizzard and have a look around."

Her smile grew teasing. "Or maybe some gorgeous woman will book a room at the inn and you'll fall head over heels in love with her.''

Chuckling at the outrageous notion, he shook his head. "My, but you are full of the romantic tonight. Must be all these valentine decorations and that crazy disco ball shining down on us. Or is there a full moon?''

"I feel restless, unsettled. Maybe I'll take a trip somewhere warm, like the Bahamas or Hawaii. Who knows? I could meet the man of my dreams.''

"True. Or you could open up your front door one day and he could be standing there.''

But Allison, who had already planted herself on a sandy beach thousands of miles from home, didn't hear a word he said.

"WHAT ON EARTH are you up to now, Pete Taggart?'' Maddy wanted to know, taking off her black wool coat and hanging it in the hall closet. She patted the tail-wagging dog. "You could hardly wait to leave the dance and get home, though you must have told me a hundred times what a great time you were having. And then to top it off, you drove like a maniac to get here. And since everyone knows you're Mr. Safety when it comes to driving, well, I just think something's up and you're not telling me.'' She crossed her arms over her chest, waiting for him to deny it.

Pete didn't bother to try. He stared at her in amusement and shook his head. "It amazes me that you can say so much and not take one breath of air. You must have amazing lung capacity.''

She followed him to the foot of the stairs. ''Don't try to change the subject. You've been acting odd all evening.''

He grinned, then scooped her up in his arms, despite her squeal of protest. ''If I am, it's because I'm crazy in love with you, Mrs. Taggart, and I can't think clearly or behave rationally when you're around.''

''I love you, too—'' she kissed his cheek ''—and you're very sweet. But you'd better put me down or you're going to break your back. I'm not exactly a lightweight anymore.''

He marched up the stairs as if she weighed no more than a feather. ''I've carried grain and feed bags all my life, babe, and you're no heavier than they are.''

She couldn't quite decide whether or not to be insulted. ''I'm not sure I like being compared to a sack of grain.''

When he reached the top landing, he didn't turn toward their bedroom as she was expecting, but rather walked farther down the hall toward the guest room. ''Where are we going, if you don't mind my asking?''

''I do mind. Now be quiet or you'll spoil the surprise.''

''Surprise? But, Pete, you've already given me this lovely diamond heart for a Valentine's Day present—'' her hand went to her throat ''—and I don't think—''

''Shh!'' he said, before he kissed her to silence, then set her down on her feet gently. ''Did anyone ever tell you that you talk too much?''

She shook her head and smiled. ''No.''

He opened the door to the guest room. ''Now close your eyes, and don't look until I tell you to.'' He guided her forward, until she was standing in the center of the room. ''Okay, you can look now.''

''You've moved all the furniture. But why?'' And then she saw it. The white baby crib and dressing table, and her eyes widened and filled with tears. She walked forward, noting the whimsical animal mobile hanging over the crib, the yellow diaper pail, the cradle he had so lovingly restored by the fireplace and the rocker next to it.

Her throat clogged with emotion. ''Oh, Pete! It's so lovely. Thank you!'' She threw her arms about his neck and kissed him. ''But when did you do it? How did you do it?''

Pete smiled secretively. ''I have my ways.'' And two brothers who were only too happy to help.

''I don't know what to say.''

''I knew you'd want to pick out the colors and stuff yourself, so I tried to get things that were neutral, except for the diaper pail. Yellow was the only color they had left, but I figured that was safe since we don't know if it's a boy or a girl.''

Feeling overwhelmed with emotion, she lowered herself onto the rocker, and it was then she saw the old patchwork quilt resting in the bottom of the cradle. It was faded from many washings, but still lovely. "Oh, this is beautiful." She picked it up, handling it with reverence.

"It was mine. Mom saved it, along with a bunch of my baby clothes. She did that for all three of us boys."

"I wish I'd known your mom, Pete. She sounds so wonderful."

"She was a neat lady. I miss her. After John set up his practice in town, and Mark bought the inn, it was just Mom, Bethany and me for a time. Then Bethany was killed and I had Mom all to myself the last year before her death."

"How awful that you had to experience such tragedy in so short a period of time."

His eyes grew haunted with memories for a moment, and then he said, "It wasn't easy. But my mom always used to say that something good always comes out of tragedy. Even though we can't see it at the time, or know what lesson we're supposed to learn, it'll make itself known eventually." He got down on his knees before her and took her hand.

"She was right, Maddy. You came into my life and made the heartache disappear." He drew her hand to his lips and kissed each of her fingers. "I love you, Maddy."

"I know. I think I've known for an awfully long time, but I was just afraid to acknowledge it, afraid you would change your mind, or that it wouldn't be true."

He rose to his feet and pulled her up with him. "I've got another surprise for you."

She looked about. "Where? Is there more baby furniture?"

He shook his head. "It's in our bedroom."

They walked to the room next door, and he led her inside. The bedroom was lit with dozens of fragrant candles, and on the nightstand stood a wine bucket containing a cold bottle of champagne and two flutes, compliments of Mark, he told her. "Happy Valentine's Day, babe."

Maddy's eyes filled with tears. To think Pete had done all of this just for her. "All I bought you was a card."

Lying on the bed was a fire-engine-red satin negligee trimmed with lace. Pete picked it up, handing it to her. "Put this on. I'll count it as my present, okay?"

She sucked in her breath. "It's beautiful. I love it!"

He placed her hand on his crotch and she could feel his hard member straining at the zipper. "Don't keep me waiting, Maddy. I'm an impatient man."

"I won't. But first, there's a little something I want to give you." She had purchased something for him but had been too embarrassed to give it to him. Moving to the nightstand, she withdrew a small package from the bottom drawer. "I bought this on impulse, and now I'm glad I did. Open it."

Pete unwrapped the package to find the tiniest pair of men's briefs he'd ever seen. His eyes widened.

They weren't just tiny, and they weren't just red, they were decorated with little white hearts, a larger one over the crotch. "Uh, they're—uh—"

She laughed at his embarrassment. "Put them on while I'm in the bathroom. I've been having all kinds of fantasies, wondering what you would look like in them."

"But they're red!" No self-respecting male wore red underpants!

"I know," she said with a grin. "We'll match."

Maddy came out of the bathroom fifteen minutes later and caught Pete staring at himself in the mirror. By the horrified expression on his face, she could tell he was not as enraptured by the sight of himself as she was. "Wow! You look—what is the word? Well hung."

His face turned as red as his briefs, and she laughed. "I feel like one of those exotic male dancers."

"Hmm," she said, reaching for the pile of bills on the dresser Pete had discarded earlier and extracting a five. "I believe this is what all the women do." She tucked the money into his crotch, allowing her hand to linger over the ridge of his erection.

"Maddy!" Pulling her to his chest, Pete planted his mouth on hers and guided her gently toward the bed. "Do women really get turned on by seeing men in these skimpy getups?" he asked, lowering the straps of her nightgown and baring her breasts to his view. "I'd much rather look at these babies."

He palmed the swollen mounds, making her cry out.

"Your breasts are so responsive. Your nipples get hard just by my looking at them," he said, lowering his head. "Imagine what they'd do if I licked them." And then he showed her.

Maddy clutched Pete's head while he suckled, then moved to discard the sexy briefs he wore and did the same to him, first licking his nipples, then dipping her tongue into his belly button, and finally slipping lower to take him full into her mouth.

"Oh, babe, you're killing me!"

When he couldn't stand the exquisite torture a moment more, he pushed her onto her back and covered her body with his. "I love you, Maddy, and I always will," he whispered, then made sure she was ready before entering her.

Welcoming Pete inside her, Maddy took his words into her heart and soul, and knew in that moment that they had been destined for each other.

Whether it had been fate, or the quilt legend, or God's doing, she didn't know. She knew only that she loved him, and that no matter what happened in the future, she always would.

Chapter Fourteen

March roared in like a lion, bringing with it gale-force winds and spitting cold rain. But despite the nasty weather, Maddy was determined to get her new business off the ground before one more day had passed.

She'd waited long enough for Pete to come around to her way of thinking, and she realized now after their conversation of this morning that he wasn't likely to ever agree with her decision to return to work.

They'd been in the middle of what she considered to be a heated discussion when the phone rang. Their neighbor, Bob Duggan, had called asking for help. The roof on his barn had blown partially off, due to the high winds, and his hay was getting soaked.

Knowing the problem had to be dealt with immediately or the hay would rot, Pete wasted no time in donning his heavy parka and gloves and was about to leave for the neighboring ranch when he stopped dead in his tracks and turned to face his wife.

"I think you should reconsider your idea of opening up your own business, Maddy, especially with the baby coming. It's not a wise decision right now, and I'm not in favor of your working while you're pregnant.

"And, don't forget, Mary Beth's likely to need your help with her baby. Trust me, you'll have plenty to keep you busy."

Maddy fought to keep her anger in check. "I've thought long and hard about this, Pete, and I'm determined to do it. And throwing my sister into this mess isn't going to change my mind. My career's important to me. If you weren't so hardheaded and opinionated you'd see that." How could she make her feelings any plainer?

She couldn't.

Pete just refused to listen.

Sighing deeply, his frustration evident, Pete glared at her, then shook his head. "We'll talk more about this tonight. I promised Bob I'd be right over, and I don't want to keep him waiting. This barn business is important."

And her career wasn't? Was that the conclusion she was supposed to draw?

Maddy nodded, even forced a smile like the good little obedient wife Pete thought she was, and then realizing that her husband was doing to her what her father had always done to her mother, she'd grown angry and more determined than ever to show Pete that she wasn't weak, that she wouldn't be manipulated, and that she had no intention of giving up her career to please him.

And so, as soon as he stepped out the door, she headed for the telephone to set her plans into motion.

An hour later, Maddy was showered, dressed and ready to meet Sweetheart's business community. But first, she had to find the keys to the tank.

"Where did I put those infernal car keys?" she asked herself, searching frantically through her purse, scouring the hall table, and finally finding them in the ceramic fruit bowl on the kitchen table. For a moment, she'd entertained the thought Pete might have hidden them from her, then felt foolish and ashamed that she'd suspected him.

Bad enough one of them was behaving somewhat underhanded, Maddy thought, a twinge of guilt tugging at her conscience. But dammit! She'd made her feelings clear from the first moment they'd discussed marriage. She had no reason to feel dishonest, guilty or anything else.

"I've got the keys, Rufus," she told the dog, who responded with a mournful whine and thumping tail before loping to the door. Rufus was ever hopeful that he would get to go bye-bye.

"You can't come this time, love. It's raining too hard, and I need to concentrate on my driving." The lovable mutt had a penchant for licking faces at the most inopportune moments, and Maddy couldn't afford any distractions. Not with the weather so bad and driving conditions treacherous. "Next time, okay?'' The dog skulked off, tail between his legs, not believing a word she said.

The rain poured down as if the heavens had opened up, and Maddy drove slowly and cautiously as she made the drive to town, trying to skirt large puddles of standing water and staying on the secondary roads to avoid traffic. Though it was late morning and not too congested, she still didn't want to take any chances.

When she reached Sweetheart's town limits without incident, she breathed a sigh of relief, then chided herself for being so silly. She used to take the New York subway, for heaven's sake! Driving twelve miles to a sleepy burg like Sweetheart was a piece of cake compared to that.

Her first stop was Windsor's Realty. She had phoned Patty Windsor earlier that morning, and the real estate agent had promised to leave keys for a vacant Main Street storefront rental at the front reception desk.

The rental was only a few doors down from the Realtor's office, so Maddy decided to brave the downpour and walk. It was impossible to use the umbrella—the wind was blowing far too hard for that.

In the short time it took Maddy to reach her destination, she became drenched. Her feet were squishing in her shoes, and her hair was plastered to her head.

Stepping inside, she flicked on the overhead lights, and a puddle of water formed at her feet. The roof wasn't leaking, so she knew the water had come from her shoes and clothing. The distinctive odor of wet wool rose up to greet her, and she wrinkled her nose at the musty smell and hoped that she hadn't ruined the floor covering. Fortunately, the light-colored carpeting looked sturdy and in pretty good condition, despite the soaking.

Walking about the empty store, Maddy had no trouble imagining her work area, a reception desk, couch, copier and fax machine. "This could work nicely," she told herself, gazing down at the listing paper she held. The rent was within her budget, too, which made it even more attractive.

Suddenly there was a loud banging on the window, and she glanced up to find Allison Montgomery, looking somewhat like a drowned rat, motioning frantically at her from the sidewalk. With a wave, she invited her inside.

"What on earth are you doing in town on a day like this, Maddy?" Allison wanted to know, shaking out her plastic rain bonnet. "Have you lost your mind completely? And look at you—your feet are soaking wet. You're going to catch a chill."

What was it, Maddy wondered, that brought out the mother hen in everyone where she was concerned? "Good morning, Allison, or should I call you Mother?" she said, smiling at the woman she now considered her best friend. "And before you continue your lecture, I'd like to point out that you're not exactly dry as a bone."

"I'm not pregnant. I'm not the one who needs to

be careful of her health and that of her unborn child.''

Maddy heaved a sigh. Though Allison meant well, her solicitousness was getting to be as annoying as Pete's. Why did everyone have to treat her like a mindless invalid, for heaven's sake? ''For your information, I came to town to take a look at what might be my new office space.''

The woman's blue eyes widened. ''So Pete finally agreed to your opening up the business? That's great, Maddy! I'm so happy for you.'' Allison's smile was genuine, and Maddy felt a tad guilty for having misled her.

''Well, not exactly,'' she confessed. ''But I've decided to go ahead and do it anyway. I love Pete, but I also love my work, and I just can't give it up totally.''

Allison digested the information but decided not to comment. Maddy had made her decision and now she would have to live with it. She hoped only that Maddy had made the right one. Allison had come to look upon her as the sister she'd never had.

''This used to be Forrest Helmsley's T-shirt store,'' Allison explained. ''But the poor guy went belly-up about six months after he opened. He's working at the auto repair shop with his dad now.''

Maddy hated to see any struggling business fail. Like many small towns, Sweetheart's downtown area was in dire need of revitalization. Some paint, new street lamps and sidewalk repair would go a long way in attracting new business owners and out-of-town visitors. Now that she was planning to invest her own resources here, Maddy would do her best to make that happen.

"That's too bad," she said finally. "Wasn't there a market for his shirts?"

"Not really. His mother, Vivian, used to hawk them at her Tupperware parties, but no one liked them much. The printed sayings were far too pessimistic. Stuff like, Repent, The End Of The World Is Upon Us, and then he'd have a picture of the world blown to smithereens." She shook her head. "Forrest always tended to look on the dark side of things. Of course, with a mother like Vivian, who could blame him?" Allison said uncharitably.

Putting her plastic rain hat back on, Allison said, "If you're done looking at the place, Maddy, let's go next door to Rose's Café and get some coffee and a muffin. I'm starving and cold, and a cup of hot coffee would go a long way to warming me up."

Maddy didn't believe for a second that her friend didn't have more to say about her decision to go forward with her business plans. "And you want to lecture me some more, right?"

Linking her arm through Maddy's, Allison smiled. "You and that husband of yours are more alike than I care to admit, my friend. Stubborn to the core. I'm done lecturing. It's your life."

"But you think I'm making a big mistake?" Maddy asked, once they were seated at a table inside the warm restaurant. She had slipped off her wet shoes, hoping her nylons would dry out. Her toes were well past the frozen point.

"Hey, I'm on your side, toots. I just don't want to see anything bad happen to you and Pete. I think you make a great couple."

"Nothing's going to happen. He'll come around to my way of thinking eventually. I'm sure of it."

Not feeling half as confident as Maddy sounded, Allison began pulling apart the blueberry muffin. "Where's Pete now? How did you escape his clutches?"

"You're making him sound like my jailer, and Pete's not like that at all. He's just…overprotective." *Overbearing. Oversolicitous.* "He went to the Duggans' ranch to help Bob repair his barn roof. The wind tore most of the shingles off and his hay was getting ruined."

Sipping her coffee, Ally pondered the wisdom of what she was going to ask, then went ahead, despite her reservations. "So tell me, Maddy, what can you do for my catering business? Do you think you could devise a plan that would get me more customers?"

At the unexpected question, Maddy's face grew animated, then her eyes widened suddenly, and her mouth formed an O. "Oh. Oh!"

"What is it? What's wrong?"

"The baby just kicked, and it was a good one. Must be a boy, huh?"

Ally leaned toward her. "Can I feel it? Would you mind?"

They were alone in the restaurant, so Maddy didn't

mind at all, and she took the woman's hand and placed it on her abdomen. "Go ahead. Feel to your heart's content."

"It's moving," the young woman said, clearly awestruck. "How wonderful. I can't wait to have a baby inside of me."

"Yes, it is wonderful. And I'm excited to have this baby. But I'm also excited to hear that you might want my help in getting Ally's Catering off the ground."

"Business isn't great," Allison admitted, her frown producing tiny lines at the bridge of her nose. "I don't think there's a lot of need for a catering service in a town this size. Maybe I should just forget it."

Maddy took a small notebook from her purse. "Nonsense! Sweetheart's large enough for your services. What you need is a brochure, something that will tell potential customers what it is that you're offering and how much it's going to cost them."

"But who would I give these brochures to?"

"Well, the high school is always having events. There are the junior and senior proms, graduation, sports awards banquets." Maddy's eyes brightened. "And there'll be times when Mark can use your help with weddings and other big events. Then there are the realty offices. They usually hold Christmas parties and open houses, and—"

"Goodness, Maddy! I hadn't thought of any of that. My business could be a real gold mine, if you'd be willing to help me."

"Of course, I'll help you. That's what I'm good at. And I'll even give you a reduced rate."

"You made a lot of money doing this in New York, didn't you?"

Proud of the fact that she'd risen high in the ranks of the prestigious advertising firm where she'd worked, Maddy nodded. "My salary was usually six figures, plus bonus. But," she emphasized, "everything's a trade-off. I had no life to speak of."

Hearing only the positive, Ally's jaw unhinged. "Wow! Six figures. Are you sure you don't want to return there? You'll never make that kind of money here, I'm afraid."

"I don't need to. I'm doing this more for my own satisfaction. I saved a lot of money during the years I worked. Couple that with the investments I made during the present bull market, and I'm pretty well-off financially."

"Does Pete know he's married to a wealthy woman?"

Maddy couldn't help the laughter that bubbled up in her throat. "He knows a little of what I have, but I didn't want to take the chance of bruising his ego by dumping too much on him all at once. And I'd appreciate it if you would keep my confidence. And that includes not telling John."

Allison stiffened at the mention of the man's name. "I haven't seen much of Dr. Taggart lately, so you needn't worry."

Surprised by her statement, Maddy sensed Ally

wasn't telling her everything. "Why's that? I thought you two were close."

She shrugged, her eyes clouding with pain. "I'd rather not talk about it, if you don't mind."

"Well, I guess I don't need to ask if you'd like to accompany me to the veterinary clinic then, do I? I have an appointment with John at three o'clock to discuss advertising for his animal clinic. Guess I'll do a bit of shopping for the nursery before then." And she wanted to go back to the realty office and fill out the forms to lease her new office space.

At the mention of the time, Ally glanced at her watch. "I've got to get back to work. I don't have a lot of business, but what I have needs to be taken care of. Namely, Owen Slattery's birthday party. The six-year-old kid wants a Star Wars spaceship cake." The caterer made a face. "I'm gonna stick it to Phyllis Slattery for putting me through so much trouble. The cake's going to be a nightmare to construct and decorate."

"I'd better get going, too," Maddy said. "I've got plenty to do, and I want to finish up and get home before Pete does."

PETE RETURNED HOME that same afternoon to find the house dark and Rufus begging to be let out. The Expedition had not been parked in its usual place, and his worst fears were realized when he entered the kitchen to find a note stuck to the refrigerator.

"Gone to town. Be back around four. Love, Maddy."

Pete plowed agitated fingers through his damp hair. "Dammit, Maddy! Why in hell did you drive to town on a day like this?" It was still raining hard and visibility had worsened due to the approach of evening.

Helping Bob with his roof during the height of the storm had been bad enough, but that was nothing compared to the nightmare he'd just come home to.

Remembering that his wife had once attempted to drive during the height of a blizzard, he swore a blue streak. Glancing at his watch, his frown deepened. Maddy was late. Only by ten minutes. But she was still late.

Pete began to pace, and the spacious kitchen soon started to feel like a jail cell. His gut churned with worry, and his heart filled with fear as he considered all the variables.

Maddy was a terrible driver. She didn't know the roads that well. What if something had happened to her on the way home? What if the car had broken down? Okay, so it was new. But it might be a lemon.

Or maybe she'd run out of gas. Or maybe she was lost. He glanced down at the table to find her cell phone there and cursed again.

He didn't want to acknowledge the worst, didn't want to contemplate the possibility, but finally he had to.

What if she'd had an accident?

He shut his eyes, unwilling to believe that God would be that cruel. Not twice in one lifetime. "Please, Maddy, come home to me."

Just then, the phone rang, and his stomach heaved as he reached for it, practically yanking it off the wall. "Maddy?"

"No, Pete. It's John."

The relief he expected to feel wasn't there. "John, this isn't a good time. Maddy's gone, and—"

"That's why I'm calling. I don't want to alarm you, but—"

Fear for Maddy's safety clawed at his heart, ripped at his soul. "What is it? What's happened? Did Maddy have an accident?"

"Calm down, will you? Now listen. Maddy didn't have an accident." The relief he felt at those words was short-lived. "But she is in the hospital."

"The hospital?" Pete felt his knees weaken, and he leaned back against the counter for support. "Is it the baby?"

"I don't know. It might be. You need to get down here right away. Dr. Peterson is with her now, performing the examination. Maddy's upset, and she's been asking for you."

Pete swallowed his panic. "I'll be right there."

Fifteen minutes later, Pete rushed through the doors of Sweetheart General Hospital and entered the emergency room. Sixteen minutes later he found his wife.

Dr. Peterson had just completed the examination and was writing something down on her chart when he burst into the lemon-colored examining room. "Maddy!" He rushed to the bed to find her pale but smiling at the sight of him.

"Pete, I'm so glad you're here."

"Dr. Peterson—" he glanced up at the physician "—what's wrong? Is Maddy going to be all right?"

"I'm fine, Pete," Maddy said to reassure him, her voice still shaking from the ordeal. "The baby's fine, too."

He breathed a sigh of relief. "Thank God! I was frantic when I arrived home and you weren't there. Then John called and—" He shook his head and kissed her. "Thank God you're okay, sweetheart."

Maddy tried not to drown in her own guilt, but the look in Pete's eyes had her throat clogged with tears.

"Maddy had some cramping today, Pete. Naturally, I was concerned when John called, and I told him to bring her right down to the emergency room."

He gazed at his wife, his forehead wrinkled in confusion. "John? I don't understand."

"I was visiting John at the animal clinic when I started to feel light-headed," Maddy explained. "Then the cramping began, and I got scared. But your brother kept his head and called Dr. Peterson." He held her gaze for several moments, then redirected his attention to the doctor.

"Maddy's going to be just fine, but I want to keep her overnight for observation, just to be certain," Laura Peterson told him. "There are admitting and insurance forms that need to be taken care of. They're waiting for you at the front desk. Why don't you go and take care of that, while I get Maddy admitted to a room for the night."

Pete squeezed his wife's hand. "I'll be right back,

sweetheart," he promised, kissing her brow. "I love you, Maddy."

"I love you, too, Pete. Please, would you tell John...tell him I said thank you. He was so good during all of this, and I think I scared him half to death."

"Of course. But tell me, what were you doing at John's office? Rufus was home when I got there, so I know it didn't have anything to do with him."

Maddy swallowed, and she started to feel sick to her stomach again. With far more bravado than she felt, she replied, "I had an appointment to discuss advertising for his business. I told you quite some time ago that John is one of my clients."

Pete tamped down the sudden spurt of anger that rose to the forefront. Despite everything he had told Maddy, asked of her, she'd gone against his wishes. "That's right, you did. Well, I'll just go and tell my brother how *grateful* we both are to him." He practically spit out the word.

She tugged on his hand. "Don't be mad at John. It wasn't his fault." She'd never forgive herself if she caused trouble between Pete and his brother.

But Pete said nothing as he exited the room, and Maddy knew that his angry silence didn't bode well.

"Pete," John said, rising to his feet as the man approached. Concern glittered in his eyes. "How's Maddy? Is she going to be okay?"

"She's going to be fine, no thanks to you."

"What the hell's that supposed to mean? I called Dr. Peterson as soon as she began to cramp. She shouldn't have been out in the damp weather, but she was so enthusiastic about starting her new business, and—''

''And you thought you'd just help her along by being one of her clients, is that it?''

''You can't keep Maddy on a leash, Pete. She's a grown woman, and she knows her own mind. If it wasn't me, it would have been someone else. She's determined to continue her career in advertising.''

''How could you do this to me, John? You knew my feelings about her working. You knew what happened to Bethany and the baby. How could you do this?''

''I didn't do anything, Pete. You're being unreasonable and hardheaded as usual. Maddy asked me if I needed help with my advertising, and I said yes. She said you and she had discussed her working, and that you'd come to an agreement about it. Had you? Had you come to an agreement about her working?''

Pete shrugged off his brother's hand. ''No! Yes! Sort of.''

''What the hell does that mean? You either discussed this issue or you didn't. According to Maddy, you and she discussed the whole issue of her working before she agreed to marry you. Is that true?''

''Yes, dammit! It's true. But I—'' Pete slumped down in one of the vinyl waiting room chairs. ''I told her we'd work it out, but I wasn't entirely truthful. I don't want her to work. Especially now that she's pregnant.''

''You don't want...'' John shook his head, his face

a mask of disgust and disappointment. "Did you ever consider what Maddy might want? She had her career long before she ever had you, bro. And if you don't smarten up, you're going to lose the best thing that's ever happened to you."

"I won't lose Maddy," Pete insisted, as if saying the words would make it so. "I love her too much. And she loves me."

"Pete, you've got to learn to bend a little, make compromises. Times are different now. Men don't rule the roost, like when dad was alive."

"That may be true. But Maddy's my wife and I've got to do what I think is best. And working while she's pregnant is not at all in her best interest."

"Pete, please be reasonable."

"You're not to discuss advertising with her again, do you hear me?"

John heaved a disheartened sigh. "I hear you, and I think you're an absolute fool. When Maddy finds out that you're warning her clients off, she won't react kindly."

"As far as I know, you and Mark are her only clients," Pete said. "I intend to tell Mark the same thing I just told you. As my brothers, I'll expect you to abide by my wishes."

John studied the stubborn set of his brother's chin, the determined glint in his eyes, and knew that arguing any further would be pointless. If there was a more stubborn man on the face of the earth, he hadn't met him.

"You're a fool, bro. Remember I told you that when all hell breaks loose."

Chapter Fifteen

Pete hadn't uttered so much as a protest regarding Maddy's leasing of the office space or her previous appointment with his brother since finding out about both events the week before. If anything, he'd been kinder and more considerate, and she felt confident and enthused that things were going to work out between them regarding the opening of her business and her plan to go back to work.

Romantically things couldn't have been better, either. Pete had been tender and solicitous during their lovemaking, kissing her senseless, telling her how much he loved her, showing her in ways she'd only dreamed about that he truly cared. This morning had been no different, and she sighed at the memories they'd created, smiling happily to herself.

Her life was on the verge of perfect. And would be, just as soon as she got her business matters settled.

With that in mind, the first person she phoned that Monday morning was Dr. John Taggart.

"Hello, John, this is Maddy."

"Maddy, it's good to hear your voice. How... how's everything going?" Did he sound odd, or was that just her imagination?

"Fine. Listen, I was hoping to reschedule our previous appointment for this afternoon, and—"

"This afternoon?" The voice on the other end of the line began to stammer, then hesitated, not sounding at all like the John she knew. "Uh, Maddy, I don't think that's going to work out for me."

"Okay. Well, how about tomorrow?"

"No good, either. Listen, why don't I just call you when I have the time? I'm a bit swamped right now, and well—I'd just as soon put this off, if you don't mind."

Disappointment washed over her as she hung up, knowing she'd just been given the brush-off, though in a very nice way. Well, sometimes clients got cold feet, she told herself. Once John had time to think about it, realized the benefits of what she could deliver, he'd come around. She was sure of it.

Searching through her Rolodex, she found Mark's number at the inn and dialed. The innkeeper had told her only two weeks before how anxious he was to get his advertising and promotion campaign going. She had come up with some wonderful ideas for how he could expand business and couldn't wait to share them.

But the conversation with the innkeeper sounded almost identical to the one she'd had with his brother. Though apologetic, Mark was too busy to see her.

Money was tight, and he wasn't sure he could afford to invest in any advertising right now. He'd have to put it off for a while.

Maddy replaced the receiver, stared at it in confusion, and felt as if she'd just had the rug pulled out from under her.

Her first two clients and they both wanted to cancel?

Something didn't feel right, didn't smell right. In fact, something smelled suspiciously like a rat.

Deciding to confront the issue head-on, Maddy dialed the one person she could count on. Allison would know what was going on, and she would tell her the truth.

"Hey, Ally, it's me. I need to ask you something."

"Guess you've already spoken to John, huh?" There was sadness and apology in the woman's voice, and Maddy's heart did a downward spiral as she began to suspect the worst.

"Well, yes. Both he and Mark gave me the brush-off, and I wondered if you knew why?"

"Don't you know, Maddy? Can't you figure it out? I tried to warn you, but you wouldn't listen."

Maddy felt the air rush out of her lungs as her suspicion took shape. "Pete?"

"I'm sorry, toots. Both John and Mark called the other day and told me that Pete had been adamant that they not pursue a business arrangement with you. I told them they were nuts, that I was still intending to use you for my catering service, but they wouldn't budge. Apparently Pete put the fear of God into them.''

Maddy's heart twisted painfully. Pete's betrayal was almost too much to bear. ''My husband's good at that.'' Tears filled her voice. ''I've got to go, Ally. I'll call you next week, and—''

''Maddy, I don't like the sound of your voice. Don't do anything rash, please! Remember, you just got out of the hospital. It's not good to upset yourself. Damn! I'm sorry. I shouldn't have said anything.''

''Don't be sorry, Ally. This isn't your fault. And things were bound to come to a head sooner or later. I was just fooling myself into thinking Pete had accepted things.''

''Where is your husband? Why isn't he there with you now?''

''Pete drove to town to pick up feed, said he had some shopping to do.'' Of course, who knew if that was even true. ''He won't be back for a while.'' Which would suit her plans just perfectly.

''Are you going to be okay by yourself? Want me to come over? We can commiserate over a quart of pralines and cream ice cream.''

She didn't want to involve Allison any more than she had already. ''No, thanks, Ally. I'm fine. And thanks for being honest with me. I'll talk to you soon.''

And then Maddy hung up, rushed upstairs and packed her suitcase.

MADDY'S TRIP TO LEADVILLE had been uneventful. The sun was shining, the wind wasn't howling, and she made very good time. The tank had handled surprisingly well, for a tank!

But even with all that, she couldn't help the feeling of relief that washed over her when she spotted her sister's brick house nestled amid the tall pine trees. It looked warm and welcoming, and right now, she needed a little of both.

Mary Beth wasn't likely to approve of her running away, but Maddy doubted her sister would refuse her refuge. And that's what she needed—to hide, to heal, to forget all about Pete Taggart and his deceitful ways. To forget that she loved him with all her heart and soul.

Banging the brass knocker, she waited several moments for Mary Beth to answer the door, to call out "I'm coming! Hold your horses," like she always did, but only silence greeted her.

"Come on, Mary Beth! You've got to be home." Maddy hadn't planned for this eventuality, and she started to panic. What if Mary Beth and Lyle had taken a trip? What if they weren't coming home? Good grief. She'd never even considered that possibility. Did she have enough money for a motel room and meals? She'd left in such a hurry this morning that she hadn't taken the time to think things through carefully. No surprise there!

Banging the knocker a few more times, she prayed. And just when she thought she would freeze to death if she remained on the porch even one more second, the front door opened.

But it wasn't Mary Beth or Lyle who greeted her, and her heart went straight to her throat.

"Dad?" She was stunned by the sight of the face she hadn't seen in years. Andrew Potter looked like a feeble old man standing there in the familiar red-and-blue-checked flannel shirt he was fond of wearing. The scent of Old Spice wafted through the screen door, stirring up memories, not all of them bad.

"Maddy? Is that you?" His eyes widened in disbelief, his wrinkled face, which had always reminded Maddy of tanned leather, eased into a smile of pure joy. "Come in here, girl. I can hardly believe these tired old eyes."

Not having much choice, Maddy entered the house, though she felt as if she'd just entered her worst nightmare. First Pete, now her father. She was batting a thousand today. Pasting on a smile and trying to hide her discomfort, she said, "Hello, Dad. You're looking well."

Reaching out, Andrew Potter wrapped his arms about his youngest daughter and gave her a heartfelt hug. His arms felt surprisingly strong, familiar and comforting, just as Maddy had remembered and, despite her urge to pull back, to distance herself from him, she remained in his embrace.

"I've missed you, Maddy. I never thought to set eyes on you again. Can you ever forgive a foolish old man who never quite got his priorities straight?"

She leaned back, searched his face and was surprised to find he was deadly serious in his apology. The sadness and remorse glittering in his eyes was genuine. "I think it's a bit premature to talk of forgiveness, Dad. We haven't seen each other in years, and well—" She just couldn't handle this right now. Not on top of everything else that had happened.

"Come in and warm up by the woodstove. You're half-frozen." She removed her heavy coat, and his eyes widened. And then he grinned. "Well, Lord have mercy! You and your sister are just full of surprises. Here I was excited at the thought of my first grandchild, and now I'm gonna have me two. Isn't that something?" He chuckled, pleased at the prospect of becoming a grandfather, surprising Maddy with his reaction. Apparently, Mary Beth had already told him of her marriage to Pete.

She moved to the woodstove to warm her hands and backside, while he eased himself onto the floral sofa. "Where's Mary Beth?" she asked, wondering when his hair had turned so white, when his hands had gotten so gnarled. "I expected to find her home."

"Lyle took her shopping. He's been working a lot of hours lately and wanted to do something nice for her. So they went to the mall, looking for things for the baby, I suspect."

She smiled at Lyle's thoughtfulness. It was just like her brother-in-law to be considerate. And then she thought of her own husband's thoughtful ways and her eyes grew teary, alarming her father.

"What's wrong, Maddy? What's got you so upset? I hope it's not the sight of me."

She shook her head. "It's nothing, Dad. Nothing that concerns you, at any rate." He looked hurt by the dismissal, and she felt immediately contrite. Pete had urged her to meet her father halfway, but her husband wasn't here to give her the moral support she needed.

"I'm sorry. It's just, my husband and I are having a disagreement, and—"

"And you ran off? That sounds too familiar, honey, I'm sad to say."

She heard the censure in his voice and stiffened. Her first instinct was to lash out, to tell him to mind his own business, but he tugged her down onto the sofa beside him, and she drew in a calming breath, waiting for him to speak.

"I know I wasn't always there for you, Maddy, and for some reason you blamed me for your mother's death."

The truth of his words hurt, and tears filled her eyes.

"I loved Sarah with all my heart and soul, you must believe me. I was just too wrapped up in playing farmer when I should have been playing the role of husband and father. When she died, I was devastated and withdrew into myself even more. It was wrong of me to do that. I should have been stronger, should have been there for you and Mary Beth.

"I never meant to neglect any of you. I never meant to drive you away, Maddy. But you ran away just the same, without ever telling me the reason, or giving me a chance to explain.''

"Oh, Dad. I—'' She couldn't deny the accusation. She had never been brave enough to discuss the problems that had existed between them. It had been easier to run away, remove herself from the unhappy situation. That had been especially true after her mother's death, which had hit her hard.

Her father had been an easy target, and she had lashed out at him, blaming and resenting him for not being able to fix things, for not being there physically and emotionally when she really needed him the most.

"You don't have to say anything, honey, but hear me out. If you love this husband of yours, then you shouldn't be running away from him. You gotta stay and work it out. That's what marriage is all about. You're expecting a child. This should be the happiest time of your life.''

Her hand covered her abdomen protectively, and she was on the verge of telling him that this wasn't Pete's child. But she couldn't. Because in all the ways that mattered, this child was more Pete's than it would ever be David Lassiter's. "Pete and I don't agree on my working and having a career. He wants me to stay at home.''

"I learned the art of compromise rather late, Maddy. But I'm thinking that there are ways that you two could work this out between you.''

Maddy explained about leasing the office space without Pete's knowledge, about his threatening his brothers if they pursued their business interests with her. "I can't tell you how hurt I was when I found out Pete went behind my back. I felt betrayed."

"And how do you think your husband felt when he found out you went behind his back and signed a lease and began seeing clients?"

"Furious, would be my guess." And just as betrayed.

"I don't know this husband of yours, but I do know that if you married him, he's got to be someone special. Someone special enough to fight for...not with." He winked at her, and she finally smiled and felt somewhat better.

"So you think I should go home and work things out?" The idea sounded awfully appealing. She had this sudden urge to throw herself into her husband's arms and tell him how very much she loved him.

Andrew shook his head, surprising her. "He'll be coming here to get you. The man's left four or five messages on your sister's machine, asking if she's seen you, wanting her to call him. Sooner or later, he'll show up. Till then, you and me need to get reacquainted. That is, if you're willing."

Maddy thought of the animosity she'd harbored toward her father all these years, how wasteful anger and hostility really were, and how much she wanted things to be different between them.

Her mother was gone, but she still had a father, if she wanted him. And she could have a grandfather for her child, if she allowed him back into her life.

Her father seemed so different than she remembered. Or was it that she hadn't allowed herself to remember anything but the bad? There'd been good times, too. Not as many, not as frequent, but they had existed.

Placing her hand in his leathery palm, she replied, "I think I'd like that, Dad," and a great burden lifted from her heart.

PETE PLACED THE RECEIVER into the cradle and sat back down at the kitchen table, feeling vastly relieved. He'd been praying long and hard to the Almighty, and those prayers had finally been answered.

"That was Maddy. She's coming home."

"Well, aren't you the lucky son of a bitch?" John told him with a sneer. "Not that you deserve another chance."

Mark agreed. "Hope you don't blow it this time. Hope you'll use your head and think before you speak. Bad enough you dragged me and John into this. Maddy probably won't even speak to us now."

His brothers weren't saying anything Pete hadn't told himself a thousand times over since coming home from town this afternoon to find his wife had left him. There'd been no note, just an empty house full of silence, the frantic barking of the dog, and a bedroom strewn with discarded clothes that wouldn't fit into the suitcase that was missing from the closet.

The pain had been such that he'd fallen onto his knees and cried. After he was finished feeling sorry for himself, he'd searched his heart and knew that he couldn't live without her. He wanted Maddy back, no matter the conditions, no matter if he had to beg.

He began making phone calls to find her. John and Mark had shown up at his door a short time later, full of contempt and anger, but also to offer their support.

John rose to his feet. "I'm just relieved she's all right. No telling what a pregnant woman will do when she's riled."

"She's bringing someone with her," Pete said. "But she didn't say who." And she didn't sound all that angry, which surprised him. Unless, of course, she had already resolved to leave him permanently and was now at peace with her decision. That possibility tore at his soul.

"Probably the sheriff," Mark said with a shake of his head. "Maddy's probably going to have you served with divorce papers."

Pete's eyes glittered dangerously, hands balled into fists, as he stood and stepped toward his youngest brother. But Mark didn't back down. Instead, he rose to his feet and stared him right in the eye. "Go ahead and hit me if you want, brother. The truth often hurts. But you've been a real ass where Maddy's concerned, and I intend to speak my mind, whether or not you like hearing what I have to say.

"That woman deserves better than the way you've been treating her, and if you don't want Maddy, then send her my way, because I'll take her off your hands. Unlike you, I know a good thing when I see it."

"Yeah, me, too," John said. "Thanks to you, Allison's not talking to me now, either."

All the anger went out of Pete, and he extended his hands in supplication. "I'm sorry, all right? I made a mistake. I admit what I did, the way I behaved, wasn't very smart. I just hope Maddy'll find it in her heart to forgive me."

"Don't tell that to us, Pete." John glanced at his watch. "You've got a few hours to get things straight in your mind before that pretty wife of yours comes home. I hope you'll do some soul-searching and reflection and make things right."

Pete nodded. "Trust me. I intend to. Just as soon as you both leave."

"I can take a hint," Mark said, reaching for his jacket. "Besides, I gotta pick the kids up at Ella's. I don't have any more time to baby-sit with my big brother." Then he grinned, wrapped his arm about Pete's neck and gave him a kiss on the cheek. "Good luck, tough guy."

Waving his brothers off, Pete returned to the house to wait. He whistled for the dog but knew he wouldn't come. Rufus hadn't wanted anything to do with him. Not since Maddy left.

The house seemed so quiet. This was what it had been like before Maddy had entered his life, bringing her smiles, her infectious laughter, her bright optimistic outlook on everything.

He'd been lonely. And so very alone.

"I promise you, Maddy, that things will be different. Just give me another chance. I know we can work it out.''

Yanking his heavy coat off the brass hook in the hallway, he went outside on the front porch to sit and wait.

MADDY SAW HIM SITTING on the porch as soon as she pulled into the driveway and the headlights caught him in their beam. Her heart went into her throat at how desolate Pete looked there on the rocker, and she wanted to rush up, throw her arms about him, and never let him go. She hadn't been able to wait for Pete to come to her. She had wanted to see him too badly.

''Mighty fine house, Maddy. Looks like your husband is a good provider.''

Pete was so much more than that, and soon her father would know it, too. ''Pete's a fine man, Dad. I think you're going to like him.''

Andrew reached over and squeezed her hand. ''As long as he does right by my little girl, we'll get along just fine.''

She kissed the old man's cheek, then bolted out of the car to greet her husband, who was running the distance between the porch and the car, shouting her name.

Maddy threw herself into Pete's arms, and he lifted her off the ground, burying his head in her neck. ''Maddy, I'm so sorry. Can you ever forgive me?''

''I already have,'' she whispered.

"Sure she can, boy. She forgave me, and we had a lot more history between us."

Pete looked over his wife's shoulder to the old man who'd come up behind her; he felt Maddy's laughter against his neck. "This is Andrew Potter," Maddy explained. "My father."

Setting Maddy down to stand beside him, Pete wrapped one arm about her shoulder and extended the other to her dad. "Pleased to meet you, Mr. Potter."

"It's Andrew. And can we finish this in the house? I'm about ready to freeze my behind off. I ain't as tough as I used to be." He winked at the couple, then walked by them and into the house, where Rufus greeted him with no small amount of enthusiasm.

"When did that happen?" Pete asked, guiding Maddy to the front porch swing. They needed a few minutes to themselves.

"Dad was at Mary Beth's house when I arrived, and we...we got a few things straightened out."

"I'm glad, sweetheart. Now, can we get some things straightened out between us, too?"

She caressed his cheek, feeling the stubble of beard beneath her hand. "I'm so sorry for running off, Pete. I should have stayed and tried to compromise. I can see that now."

"Maybe you couldn't, because you were married to the hind end of a mule."

She smiled softly. "I love you, Pete, and I want to make you happy. So—"

He placed his fingers over her lips to silence her.

"I was wrong, Maddy, about a great many things. You had a successful career when I married you, and it was selfish of me to expect you to give it up. I love you, Maddy, and if working makes you happy then I want you to continue working and make a go of your business. I know it's important to you, just as important as this ranch is to me."

She was stunned and grateful for his admission, and it made what she had to say a lot less difficult. "Thank you for saying that, and for meaning it this time. But I've been doing a lot of thinking, and I don't see any reason why I couldn't run my business out of the house. Plenty of people work from home, and there's no reason why I can't, too."

His face brightened instantly. "That's great! But only if you're sure that's what you want to do. I don't want you working at home just because you think it's what I want."

"If we're going to be married for as long as I'm planning we will, Mr. Taggart, then I think we're both going to have to learn the art of compromise. I was very good at working things out, solving difficult situations when I worked, in order to make all the parties involved happy. I don't see the difference in doing the same with my marriage, especially since it's a whole lot more important to me than my career."

The front door opened and Maddy's father stuck his head out. "You two kids going to jaw all night, or are you coming inside to keep an old man company? I figured you've already kissed and made up by now. And if you haven't, then what are you waiting for?'' The door closed again, and Pete threw back his head and laughed.

"I think I'm going to like your father.''

"Me, too,'' admitted Maddy.

"Although,'' Pete said, looking concerned, "how are we supposed to—'' He rolled his eyes. "You know? With him in the house.''

Now it was Maddy's turn to giggle. "He goes to bed quite early, and he's a very sound sleeper.''

"In that case, Mrs. Taggart, you'd better kiss me and be quick about it. I've missed you like crazy, and I'm going to die if we don't go upstairs and make love right this minute.''

Maddy looked toward the door, where her father had stood just moments before, then toward the car. A wicked gleam entered her eyes. "I was thinking, Pete, that the tank is awfully roomy. And I believe *Consumer Reports* rated the suspension as one of the best.''

He grinned. "And what'll we do to keep warm, sweetheart, while we're testing out the suspension?''

"Why, Mr. Taggart,'' she said, drawing his lower lip between her teeth and nibbling, "you're an Eagle Scout. I'm sure you can improvise.''

And he did.

From bestselling
Harlequin American Romance author

CATHY GILLEN THACKER

comes

TEXAS VOWS

A McCABE FAMILY SAGA

Sam McCabe had vowed to always
do right by his five boys—but after
the loss of his wife, he needed the small-town security
of his hometown, Laramie, Texas, to live up to that
commitment. Except, coming home would bring him
back to a woman he'd sworn to stay away from.
It will be one vow that Sam can't keep....

On sale March 2001

Available at your favorite retail outlet.

HARLEQUIN®
Makes any time special ™

Visit us at www.eHarlequin.com

PHTV

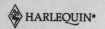
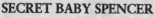

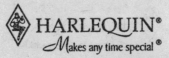

If you enjoyed what you just read,
then we've got an offer you can't resist!

Take 2 bestselling love stories FREE!

Plus get a FREE surprise gift!

Clip this page and mail it to Harlequin Reader Service®

IN U.S.A.
3010 Walden Ave.
P.O. Box 1867
Buffalo, N.Y. 14240-1867

IN CANADA
P.O. Box 609
Fort Erie, Ontario
L2A 5X3

YES! Please send me 2 free Harlequin American Romance® novels and my free surprise gift. Then send me 4 brand-new novels every month, which I will receive months before they're available in stores. In the U.S.A., bill me at the bargain price of $3.57 plus 25¢ delivery per book and applicable sales tax, if any*. In Canada, bill me at the bargain price of $3.96 plus 25¢ delivery per book and applicable taxes**. That's the complete price and a savings of at least 10% off the cover prices—what a great deal! I understand that accepting the 2 free books and gift places me under no obligation ever to buy any books. I can always return a shipment and cancel at any time. Even if I never buy another book from Harlequin, the 2 free books and gift are mine to keep forever. So why not take us up on our invitation. You'll be glad you did!

154 HEN C22W
354 HEN C22X

Name	(PLEASE PRINT)	
Address	Apt.#	
City	State/Prov.	Zip/Postal Code

* Terms and prices subject to change without notice. Sales tax applicable in N.Y.
** Canadian residents will be charged applicable provincial taxes and GST.
   All orders subject to approval. Offer limited to one per household.
® are registered trademarks of Harlequin Enterprises Limited.

AMER00   ©1998 Harlequin Enterprises Limited

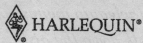

HARLEQUIN®

makes any time special—online...

eHARLEQUIN.com

your romantic life

Romance 101
♥ Guides to romance, dating and flirting.

Dr. Romance
♥ Get romance advice and tips from our expert, Dr. Romance.

Recipes for Romance
♥ How to plan romantic meals for you and your sweetie.

Daily Love Dose
♥ Tips on how to keep the romance alive every day.

Tales from the Heart
♥ Discuss romantic dilemmas with other members in our Tales from the Heart message board.

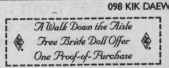

Harlequin invites you to walk down the aisle...

To honor our year long celebration of weddings, we are offering an exciting opportunity for you to own the Harlequin Bride Doll. Handcrafted in fine bisque porcelain, the wedding doll is dressed for her wedding day in a cream satin gown accented by lace trim. She carries an exquisite traditional bridal bouquet and wears a cathedral-length dotted Swiss veil. Embroidered flowers cascade down her lace overskirt to the scalloped hemline; underneath all is a multi-layered crinoline.

Join us in our celebration of weddings by sending away for your own Harlequin Bride Doll. This doll regularly retails for $74.95 U.S./approx. $108.68 CDN. One doll per household. Requests must be received no later than June 30, 2001. Offer good while quantities of gifts last. Please allow 6-8 weeks for delivery. Offer good in the U.S. and Canada only. Become part of this exciting offer!

Simply complete the order form and mail to:
"A Walk Down the Aisle"

IN U.S.A
P.O. Box 9057
3010 Walden Ave.
Buffalo, NY 14240-9057

IN CANADA
P.O. Box 622
Fort Erie, Ontario
L2A 5X3

Enclosed are eight (8) proofs of purchase found on the last page of every specially marked Harlequin series book and $3.75 check or money order (for postage and handling). Please send my Harlequin Bride Doll to:

Name (PLEASE PRINT)

Address   Apt. #

City   State/Prov.   Zip/Postal Code

Account # (if applicable)   **098 KIK DAEW**

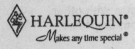

HARLEQUIN®
Makes any time special ®

Visit us at www.eHarlequin.com

A Walk Down the Aisle
Free Bride Doll Offer
One Proof-of-Purchase

PHWDAPOP